How the Earl Fell for His Countess

How the Earl Fell for His Countess

Laura A. Barnes

Laura A. Barnes

2021

First Printing: 2021

ISBN: 9798707606359

Laura A. Barnes

Website: www.lauraabarnes.com

Cover Art by Cheeky Covers

Editor: Telltail Editing

To: My Lovely Readers

Thank you for reading my stories and all your

encouraging words of support.

Cast of Characters

Hero ~ Reese Worthington

Heroine ~ Evelyn Holbrooke

Lady Worthington ~ Reese's mother

Graham (Worth) Worthington ~ Reese's brother

Eden Worthington ~ Reese's sister

Noel Worthington ~ Reese's sister

Margaret (Maggie) Worthington ~ Reese's sister

Uncle Theo ~ Duke of Colebourne

Lucas Gray ~ Colebourne's son

Jacqueline Holbrooke ~ Evelyn's sister/Colebourne's niece

Charlotte Holbrooke ~ Evelyn's twin sister/Colebourne's niece

Jasper Sinclair ~ Charlotte's husband

Gemma Holbrooke ~ Charlotte's cousin/Colebourne's niece

Abigail Cason ~ Colebourne's ward

Barbara Langdale ~ Reese Worthington's ex-mistress

Chapter One

Reese Worthington stared across the carriage at the lady who was now his wife. He didn't know what infuriated him more: the fact that she wasn't the one he thought he would wed or her casual indifference now that she wore his ring on her hand.

When he accepted the Duke of Colebourne's invitation to a house party, he'd been promised a dowry of a substantial amount if he wed one of the duke's wards. The duke had dangled the offer at him, and in return, Worthington would share his expertise on horse breeding. The duke learned that Worthington had invested a large sum in his breeding program and needed money. The program would fall by the wayside without funds. When Worthington first started the program, his father had still been alive.

Since then, his father had died, leaving Worthington's family destitute. Every shilling was spoken for, even the future profits from the breeding program and the income from the tenants. It would be years before the family's coffers were stable. His father had spent the family's fortune on gambling and whoring. Not only had his father tarnished the family's reputation with his disreputable lifestyle, but they were also feed for the gossipmongers. Worthington had hoped Colebourne's offer would elevate his family out of the rumor mill. Instead, the matter of his own marriage would send the tongues wagging.

A hasty carriage ride to Gretna Green meant one thing and one thing only. A gentleman had ruined a lady.

Could Worthington address Evelyn Holbrooke as a lady considering the events leading to their marriage? Nay, she was Evelyn Worthington now. A countess at that. He still didn't understand why Evelyn and her sister Charlotte had set out to deceive him. Why did they play their game with him? Because of their deception, he'd lost a bet that would have gained him a horse for his program.

Once the house party was underway, the duke had dangled another offer in front of the invited gentlemen. Whichever gentleman won Charlotte Holbrooke's hand would receive his prized mare, Sapphire's foal, for a betrothal present. Worthington held the belief he would be the lucky man. At every turn, he'd romanced Charlotte. They stole kisses when no one watched, their hands would intertwine during meals when they sat together. Then during the ball, he lured her into his bedroom and seduced Charlotte into giving herself to him.

~~~

"I cannot go another moment without making love to you. You are the very air I breathe," Reese had whispered to her.

A blush spread across her cheeks, drifting along her chest. Reese followed the trail with his fingers, brushing across her hardened nipples. She had sighed at his touch. He hungered for her screams.

"Please do not deny me, my love."

"I tremble from your very touch. I will surely die from the pleasure of your love," she whispered.

Reese grinned wickedly at her confession. "No. You shall only fly to heaven in my arms."

He bent his head to tempt her with a kiss, but she stepped away from him. It was then that he realized he no longer held the upper hand. He was no longer the seducer. She held all the power.

"Will you fly, too?" she whispered, undoing the buttons along the side of her dress.

Reese nodded like a bumbling fool as the dress slid off her body and landed in a heap around her. She stood before him, a goddess offering herself to him.

"No," he growled.

"No?" Confusion and doubt marred her lovely features.

Reese strode to her, lifting her in his arms. He lowered his head and ravished her mouth, leaving her no doubt of his intentions. He pulled kiss after kiss from her lips, demanding the same passion from her that consumed him.

"I shall soar."

~~~

The memories of making her his flashed through his mind. Her sighs still whispered in his ears while her silky skin caressed his body. Worthington hungered for the taste of her kiss, even now. But those memories were false. It wasn't Charlotte Holbrooke he made love to, but Evelyn Holbrooke, her twin sister. Worthington had made a promise to himself before leaving the duke's estate.

He would never forgive Evelyn for her deceit.

Because of her, he'd gained no horse to help his breeding program. Their hasty marriage would bring shame upon his family and cause his sisters' debuts to be riddled with rumors. Then there was the promise he made to himself years ago about not following in his father's footsteps.

Which now left him with a wife he refused to bed. Because of his promise to never cheat on his wife, he would find no pleasure elsewhere.

The longer Worthington stared at his wife, the more he decided he would only bed Evelyn to get her with child. After she conceived the heir and spare, he would suffer through a life of celibacy. His determination to make his wife suffer a life without husbandly attention would be his reward. Perhaps next time she would think twice before making a fool out of him.

Evelyn flipped the page of the novel she was attempting to read. She only pretended to read to show her husband his coldness didn't affect her. Ever since they left Gretna Green, his disapproving stare had been focused on her. In the past, Evelyn would have squirmed and apologized for any misgivings. However, Worthington's glare had grown wearisome. At least he gave her a reprieve from his rantings, something she'd had to endure since they left her uncle's estate during the long ride to Gretna Green. Evelyn didn't know where she gained the confidence to face the prospect of a daunting marriage, if it was from Worthington's signet ring on her finger or from pretending to be her sister Charlotte during the house party.

Evelyn understood the fault lay with her. She had wronged Worthington with her deceit. However, he wasn't the innocent gentlemen he projected himself to be. His seduction of her innocence held many faults. Even though he thought he'd seduced Charlotte, his reasoning was still cold. His only purpose was to gain a horse. A stupid horse. Every kiss, caress, and romantic words whispered were false. While Evelyn fell in love with the rake, he only used her to win a bet.

I do not focus my attention on dull debutantes.

Once he discovered her duplicity, he had made it clear how he would never choose her. She was too dull for his tastes. Evelyn remembered every hurtful remark he made in Uncle Theo's study. By then it was too late for Worthington. He had already stated his intentions, and Uncle Theo wouldn't let him withdraw his offer. To make matters worse, her family also heard Worthington's opinion of Evelyn.

Her cousin, Lucas Gray, had kept Worthington's hateful comments secret from Jacqueline, Gemma, and Abigail. At least she didn't have to suffer through their pity before she left. To them, they believed Worthington had fallen as deeply in love with Evelyn as she had with him. Uncle Theo, Lucas, and Charlotte were the only ones who knew the truth. Also, her sister's soon-to-be husband, Jasper Sinclair. At least her sister had found love at the house party. The love between Charlotte and Jasper had been in plain sight for months, but they had been too blind to see it. Her family didn't hold pity for Evelyn, only fury at Worthington's disregard toward her.

A disregard Evelyn accepted and planned to change over the course of the next few months.

Oh, it would be no easy feat. Her husband was bound and determined to make her regret her past actions. However, Evelyn planned to seduce her husband at every opportunity she got. When Reese Worthington least expected it, Evelyn would strike. Then he would have to succumb to the passion they shared. Soon Reese Worthington would declare his love for Evelyn.

Then Uncle Theodore could declare his success at two matchmaking attempts. A madness they had all declared, yet it made perfect sense.

~~~~~

Reese watched the devious smile spread across his wife's face. He knew she wasn't reading her novel. If so, she was a swift reader. She flipped a page every minute. Also, Evelyn's eyes weren't focused on the pages. They strayed away and became lost in thought before she blinked again. Reese wondered what she planned for him next. Since her sister could no longer help her, it wouldn't be anything Reese couldn't handle. Charlotte had been the mastermind of their deceit and Evelyn only a puppet. Without her sister's devious mind, Evelyn would be no match for Reese. From what he knew of his wife, she was timid, biddable, and unadventurous….and also seductive, passionate, desirable, and very kissable.

Even in this instance, Reese wanted to kiss those lips spread in a smile that would surely be his demise. He needed to get his lust under control…

Or did he? Reese had already decided he would bed Evelyn until she grew with child. Why not take her when he wanted to and purge her from his system? He had wanted her since he first kissed her over the holidays last year. Granted, he'd thought she was Charlotte, but it still hadn't stop him from fantasizing about her since then.

On the last evening of the house party, Evelyn had fulfilled every fantasy of his and created more he wished to experience. What reason did Reese have for not enjoying their wedding night at the next inn? Other than he'd been hell-bent on continuing home to rid himself of her presence. Instead, why not consummate the marriage and leave no doubt of their marriage vows? Reese wouldn't receive the dowry from Colebourne until Evelyn sent word of their marriage. He needed that money to ease his family's hardship.

Why not romance and seduce his wife this evening and every evening until she wrote to her uncle? Perhaps the old man would find it generous to send a substantial settlement. By then Evelyn might carry their child and he would have tired of her.

Reese rapped his walking stick on the carriage ceiling and informed his driver to stop at the next village.

"I thought we were continuing to your estate?" Evelyn asked.

"I realized that would be insensitive to your needs. Someone of your delicate nature should spend the night in a bed, not a carriage seat."

"Lord Worthington, I am not a delicate flower. I can handle the current accommodations if you have a need to return home immediately."

"Lady Worthington, I disagree. Your fragile frame is used to the comforts of leisure. We might have had cause for haste the past few days, but we no longer do. I have decided we can take our time before reaching your new home."

"That is very generous. My aching body thanks you." Evelyn's smile held her gratitude. A smile Reese had to harden his heart to.

At the mention of her body, Reese took in her slumped shoulders, her hair falling loose, and the dark circles under her eyes. His brutish treatment over the last few days showed on her bedraggled appearance. She had changed into a new dress before their ceremony, but there had been no one to help Evelyn with her hair. Reese had woken her before dawn from the inn and told her they were to leave in ten minutes.

Evelyn hadn't made him wait. She'd dressed hurriedly and joined him in the carriage for the hour ride into Gretna Green. It hadn't taken him long to find someone to perform the ceremony. Then he hustled her into the carriage, bent for home.

Evelyn may have been wrong with her deceit, but Reese had no reason to treat her in this manner. Not once had she complained, making his comments on her delicate nature ring false to his ears.

Reese raised his head and blew out a breath. "I am sorry for my harsh treatment. I hope a hot bath, a warm dinner, and a comfortable bed this evening might right my wrong."

If Evelyn's smile of gratitude had affected him, it held nothing compared to the smile she gifted him now. Forgiveness shone from her eyes, which also displayed her love. Reese gulped. Even though Evelyn never spoke the words, he knew the truth. It would have been the only reason Evelyn let Reese make love to her. Evelyn Holbrooke loved him. It was an emotion Reese must destroy. But not now.

Now, he would use his charm to make her believe he loved her, too.

Chapter Two

Once they arrived at the inn, Reese played the attentive husband. He procured them a suite of rooms that held its own dining area, toiletry room, and a bed fit for a king. In fact, the King of England had used it many times on his annual trip to Scotland. A more romantic atmosphere for their wedding night Evelyn couldn't have asked for. The arrangement made their hasty marriage to Gretna Green worth it. Reese announced their recent vows to the innkeeper, and they rolled out the royal treatment.

The innkeeper's wife sent a maid to help Evelyn freshen up for dinner, while Reese saw to the accommodations for the driver and the carriage. A bath awaited her when she walked into the room. She luxuriated in the bath, letting the warm water soothe her scattered emotions. Evelyn soon calmed and readied herself for a night she eagerly awaited since she pledged herself to Reese that morning.

Evelyn waited nervously by the window for Reese's arrival. A spread sat on the table for dinner with a bottle of wine ready to toast their marital bliss. A small cake sat in the center of the table. The innkeeper's gift. The older lady had gushed over what a fine couple they made. She told Evelyn how romantic Reese was when he requested their dinner and the romantic setting. She had never met more of a thoughtful husband before Reese. That Evelyn was a lucky lady indeed.

Was she? Had Reese had a change of heart since they left Uncle Theo's estate? Or would he seek his revenge another way?

In truth, Evelyn felt helpless to Reese's emotions. Even though her husband had stated what he thought of her, it still didn't stop Evelyn from loving him. Because underneath his hatefulness, she knew he desired her. And with desire came love. Evelyn held faith that the passion they shared could be nothing but love. Tonight, she would use that passion to strengthen their connection.

Reese stood in the doorway, staring at his wife. Evelyn hadn't noticed his arrival yet. He'd used another room in the inn to bathe in after their long carriage ride. He noticed his wife had made use of the luxury herself. She stood near the window, wearing a robe. From the firelight's glow, he saw not much lay underneath. Evelyn's midnight black hair cascaded to the middle of her back. A tempting package for his grounds of seduction.

By morning, his wife would understand the status of their relationship.

For now, Reese must admit that no other lady held the beauty of his wife. Not even her twin sister. After much reflection during their journey, Reese saw the differences between the sisters. Evelyn's every movement exuded gracefulness, and she held a gentleness to her touch. How did he not see the differences before? Or had he and he wouldn't admit to them? When he tried to corner Charlotte, she would brush him aside like an annoying insect. On other occasions, Reese coaxed her into sharing the sweetest of kisses, her innocence weakening his control. When he thought Jasper Sinclair and Duncan Forrester wanted her too, it'd driven him mad.

Even now a madness hovered in the air. He longed to take her. To hell with the dinner set for them. There would be time to dine later. Reese wanted to make this a wedding night Evelyn would never forget. He needed her to see what their marriage could have been if she hadn't deceived him. Reese intended to make Evelyn crave his lovemaking and understand that she would only ever receive it if he deemed it so.

Evelyn turned to find Reese standing in the doorway holding flowers. However, the flowers weren't what took her notice, but the heat flaring in his eyes. The same heat from before that melted her resistance to the pull of attraction between them. Ever since the kiss under the mistletoe, Evelyn had been unable to deny Reese.

Evelyn stepped toward him, but in three strides, Reese was before her. He threw the flowers on the chair and wrapped her in his embrace. He lowered his head and gripped her face, staring deeply into her eyes. His grip tightened, and she watched the turbulent emotions darken his gaze. Reese tried to resist the pull, but like Evelyn, he wouldn't be able to. Evelyn trailed her fingers across his cheek, her touch soft. Gentle. Coaxing.

Reese closed his eyes, trying to bring himself under control. But when he opened them again, he lost himself in Evelyn. Her entire essence surrounded him, completing him. For some unknown reason, Evelyn had felt like home to him since their first kiss under the mistletoe. A home he wanted to sink himself into and never rise from again. The madness he held onto unleashed itself at the gentle touch of her hand.

He lowered his mouth and possessed hers. Nothing gentle, but a powerful connection that he dominated. His mouth plundered hers over and over, taking and demanding everything from her. His hands slid in her hair and held her mouth to him as he drank from her sweet lips, sucking out every succulent drop until nothing but dark desire remained.

Reese's kisses demanded Evelyn's utter devotion. He controlled her senses with each stroke of his tongue. Every emotion Evelyn possessed, Reese demanded her to surrender to him. He seared a path of fire along her neck to her breasts. When he met a barrier to what he most desired, he took it upon himself to bare Evelyn before his eyes. He stripped the robe from her body, leaving her standing before him in a nightgown made of the finest silk.

Reese trailed one finger under the strap and slid it off her shoulder, then he trailed the finger back up again against her bare skin. Evelyn shivered. Not from the cold, but from the sensation of Reese's sizzling touch.

The white temptation of sin covering Evelyn left nothing to Reese's imagination. The glow from the fire highlighted every dip and curve of his wife. His devilish smile made her shake more. Reese pressed a kiss to her bare shoulder, and Evelyn shuddered at the simple gesture. His lips trailed lower to the lace covering her breasts.

He stopped, staring at the decorative buttons lining the front of Evelyn's gown. They may have been for decoration, but to Reese, they were an enticement to rip the gown from Evelyn's body. He needed to get his emotions under control. Evelyn shook his very foundation. She brought forth his fury at her betrayal, yet Evelyn revealed her vulnerability at his touch, making him protective toward her. How could a mere slip of a lady set his emotions ricocheting out of control?

Evelyn stood still, confused by why Reese had stopped. His hands hovered over her nightgown as if he contemplated ripping the garment. When they shook, Evelyn placed her hands atop his.

"Worthington?"

He stared at their hands and didn't know who shook more. He tore his hands out from underneath hers, then ripped the front of the negligee apart. The delicate buttons scattered across the room, rolling about on the uneven floor. Evelyn stood bare before him, and her body glowed from the fire, tempting him. He pulled her flushed against him, her creamy skin silk under his touch.

She gasped when he lifted her into his arms and carried her to the bed. Before he laid her down, he whispered, "When my lips touch yours, you are to whisper my name. When my hands caress your silken skin, you are to moan my name. And when I make love to you, you are to scream my name." He touched his lips to Evelyn's. "What do you call me?"

"Reese," Evelyn whispered.

He caressed Evelyn's body, his hands brushing across her breasts, down to her stomach, lowering to her curls. Reese whispered in her ear, "What do you call me?"

Reese's hands slid between her thighs, opening her up to him. He sank his fingers into her wetness, sliding a finger inside.

"Reese." Evelyn moaned.

Reese felt himself slipping further out of control. He stroked his finger in and out of Evelyn, her wetness coating him. He lowered his head, sliding the tight bud of her nipple between his lips. Reese suckled the sweet berry as his tongue stroked back and forth. Evelyn moaned his name over and over at his attention, her fingers running through his hair, holding his head to her breasts.

Evelyn's ache grew. She needed Reese to love her now. She wanted to scream his name as he'd demanded. Evelyn lost herself to Reese at his first touch. When he flew across the room and showed her his vulnerability, Evelyn wanted Reese to take her in that moment. She moved her hips with his hand, building her desire. Her hands started clawing at his shirt to remove it. She wanted his heat to burn her. Her entire life, she had hidden in a shell, too afraid to live. Now she only wanted to fly in Reese's arms.

Reese pulled his shirt over his head, and Evelyn reached out to run her fingers down his chest, sliding them across each hardened ridge. Her hands lowered to his trousers and brushed across his hardness. He let out a hiss, drawing her gaze to his. His blue eyes darkened into sapphires. With trembling fingers, she unbuttoned the placket of his trousers. Before she could reach inside, he grabbed her arms and brought them above her head, holding her wrists with one hand.

If she touched him, he would lose the remainder of his control. Evelyn's body trembled under him with anticipation. After only having her the one night, he already knew what she craved. He knew her body better than his own.

With his other hand, he pushed his pants down and kicked them to the side. He ran his hand up her leg, pushing her thighs farther apart. He needed Evelyn now. Needed her like he needed to breathe.

Evelyn opened herself wider, hooking one of her legs around Reese's hip. The turbulence of emotion in the air clung to them, begging the storm to rage. He slid slowly inside her, dragging out each sensation of bliss. He filled her, his need throbbing, and held still. She moaned his name.

Reese listened to the moan of his name whispered from Evelyn's lips. He was between heaven and hell at this very moment. He lived in hell for his fury toward her, but her sweet body welcomed him into heaven. Her wetness tightened around him, holding him hostage. A hold that he never wanted her to release.

He stared down into her eyes, watching her emeralds darken with desire. Evelyn's need for him beckoned him closer. Her luscious breasts heaved with her need. Her nipples tightened under his stare. His gaze traveled lower to where they were connected as one.

He pulled out slowly to see how her wetness coated his cock. Evelyn arched her body, begging for him to fill her again. Reese paused, waiting for Evelyn to writhe underneath him with a need only he could fulfill. When her hips pressed into his, he could no longer hold back from fulfilling both of their desires.

He slammed into her, filling her to the brim, and whispered, "What do you call me?"

"Reese!" Evelyn screamed his name over and over each time he slid out and filled her again.

He released Evelyn's hands and held her body upright, loving her. His passion was relentless. It drew her soul away and into him. With each stroke, he slid in deeper, and his lips seared fire across her body with each nip. Evelyn screamed his name with each stroke, clinging to him with her head flung back.

"Look at me, Evelyn."

She opened her eyes and stared at him. She saw the madness in his eyes, his uncontrollable desire, and knew in that moment what he wouldn't admit to himself.

As much as he would deny it, he loved her, too.

She lifted her hand and soothed the tension away from his eyes. He closed them at her gentle touch, fighting what he saw in her stare.

Reese wanted to declare that she would never make a fool out of him again, but one touch from her and his anger fled. Anger he must cling to. After tonight, he would, but for now, he only wanted to revel in the pleasure of holding Evelyn.

He lowered his head and devoured her lips as he took their bodies over the brink of desire. When they went flying, Evelyn let forth a scream of his name that left Reese in no doubt of who he made love to this night.

Chapter Three

Reese sat dressed, watching his wife sleep. His heart tried hardening, but it kept softening every time his gaze fell upon Evelyn.

He needed to continue their trip to his estate in a hurry to escape her company. At his home, she wouldn't bother him the way she did in such close confines. He could pawn her off on his mother and siblings. And he could spend his time in the stables.

Once he received Evelyn's dowry, he would head to London to settle his accounts. During the trip, he could purchase more livestock at Tattersalls for his program. Losing out on Sapphire's offspring came as a blow, but it was one he would recover from. There were other offspring that came from excellent lines available for purchase.

Evelyn lay naked under the covers. They had spent their wedding night reaching for each other to love until the early dawn when she fell into an exhausted slumber. But not Reese. Instead, he'd watched his wife sleep. Evelyn appeared sweet and innocent. While she may have a sweet disposition, her innocence rang false. That was what Reese needed to remember. However, it was her sweetness that kept his heart from hardening.

Even now, he wanted to lift the covers and drink her in. Slip beneath them and awaken her with his body sliding into hers. Listen to her whisper, moan, and scream his name again. He wanted to learn what pleased her and teach her how to please him.

But instead, he sat there like the fool she played him to be, allowing her the rest she needed.

Evelyn stretched, her tender body protesting. She reached her arm out for Reese. She might be wanton, but she ached for him to love her again. When he made love to her, he kept his resentment at bay. While his anger dictated how he loved her, it made their lovemaking more intense.

When she felt the cool sheets, she opened her eyes and searched for Reese. She found him sitting in a chair facing the bed, staring at her. A frown rested on his face, and she realized their truce had come to an end. Her husband had returned to his resentful self.

Still, Evelyn tried to reach him. She held out her hand. "Reese?"

His dark laughter filled the room. "Madam, I have only given you leave to address me by my Christian name when I am kissing you, caressing you, or sticking my cock inside you. Since I am doing none of those acts at this time, you can refer to me as Worthington." He stood and motioned for her to rise. "I have given you ample enough time to rest. A maid will arrive with a tray for you to eat, then she will help you dress. You have one hour, then we must depart."

Reese's coldness settled over her. She wouldn't show him how it affected her. Evelyn would allow him his bitterness for a time because she still held guilt for her deception. But their marriage wouldn't stay like this forever. Evelyn had spent her life cowering from anything uneasy, hiding herself away. But she no longer wished to live her life in that regard. Reese made her feel alive. Her new agenda would be to live a full life. As Aunt Susanna always said, kill them with kindness. And in the meantime, Reese wouldn't see what was coming.

Evelyn nodded her acceptance. "Thank you for allowing me the extra hours to rest. I am most grateful. I shall be ready to leave in one hour's time."

Reese strode to the door, frustrated that Evelyn hadn't turned teary-eyed at his cruelty. Instead, she accepted it without a word of protest. Before he left the suite, her words stopped him.

"And, Worthington?"

He stood in the open doorway, facing the hallway, not wanting to see the determination he heard in her voice.

"I wait with anticipation for when I can whisper, moan, and scream your God-given name while you pleasure me with your body," Evelyn purred.

Reese gritted his teeth at the seductive sound of her voice. His wife's reply showed proof that he held no power over her.

He slammed the door and stomped down the stairs to distance himself from her. Reese needed to get himself under control before the long carriage ride ahead of him. Once he reached the dining area, he barked an order to the innkeeper at the request of a maid and ordered a bottle of brandy for the ride. Once the maid had given him one, he carried the bottle to the carriage, where he waited for his wife to join him.

Evelyn was proving to be the bane of his existence.

Evelyn sighed, rising with the blanket wrapped around her. She searched for her robe, and when she found it in the corner, she pulled it around her naked form. She took a step toward the fire and stepped on the tiny buttons of her ripped nightgown. Evelyn lowered herself to the floor, gathering as many of them as she could find.

With her hand full, she carried them to her valise, where she placed them inside. She looked around for the torn garment and couldn't find it. She lifted the covers on the bed and searched the room, only to come up empty. Reese must have discarded the garment to save Evelyn the awkwardness of explaining the reason for its destruction.

Evelyn sat on the bed, thinking over the matter of her husband. It would appear Reese had reverted to his charming self, she thought sarcastically. However, his thoughtfulness contradicted his harsh behavior. Reese was proving to be a confusing gentleman.

She laughed before she rose to get ready to leave.

~~~~~~

The carriage ride slowed to a crawl along the long driveway to his estate. Worthington swiped a hand along his face. His gritty eyes tried to open wider before they came to a stop. He sat up straighter, shaking the grogginess from his head. A weight settled against him, halting his movements. He looked down to see Evelyn snuggled against him, a blanket covering them. His wife lay curled in his lap with her head on his chest.

In his hazy drunkenness, he remembered waking up to see Evelyn asleep with her head hitting the carriage window with every bump in the road. He'd taken pity on her and lifted her to sit next to him. Her body had trembled from the cool weather. They had traveled into a light rain, leaving the air damp. Worthington settled a blanket over them and dropped his head back against the seat.

When Evelyn's body continued to shake, he'd settled her on his lap. At her sigh of contentment, he'd lifted his bottle to drink his courage of enduring the rest of the ride. He took a drink each time her curves settled against his cock. After he finished the bottle, he wrapped the blanket tighter, his hand sliding under her dress to settle between her thighs, and fell asleep. That was the last thing he remembered.

The carriage stopped, and a footman opened the door. Worthington pulled his hands from under the blanket and motioned for silence. He nodded his head for the footman to take Evelyn from his arms. Once he alighted from the carriage, Worthington looked to the stars for guidance, but he knew he wouldn't find any.

Worthington stretched and held his arms out for Evelyn. They had ridden through the night on his orders to reach home. The hour had grown past a reasonable time. The butler held the door open, and Worthington strode into the entryway.

Jenkins, the butler, held a lone candlestick in the surrounding darkness of the house. "Lord Worthington, we were not expecting you home so soon."

"Yes, well, I need a place to store my bride for the duration of my marriage," Worthington slurred, his body swaying.

"We have a new Lady Worthington?" squeaked Jenkins.

"Shh, do not wake the house with the news. I will announce my marriage in the morning. For now, my bride requires a bed, one preferably far from mine."

Worthington strode off toward the staircase with Jenkins following him, trying to keep up. However, even as drunk as he was, his long strides were no match for the aging butler. Worthington slung the door open to the bedroom for the mistress of the house. The bedroom had been closed off because of their low funds, as were most of the rooms at Worthington Hall. He had ordered the staff to cover the rooms since they couldn't afford to hire enough servants to keep them cleaned.

"Jenkins!" Worthington bellowed.

Evelyn stirred in his arms, but continued to sleep.

Jenkins arrived at his side, gasping for breath. He held his side in agony. The trek up the stairs was tiring for the butler. "On your orders, my lord. The staff closed the room. The only available bed for Lady Worthington would be yours. Shall I send for Mrs. Stickler to help the lady?"

Worthington stared at his wife and realized the torment of being in Evelyn's company would have to continue until tomorrow morning. She slept soundly. How much would she bother him, anyway? Tomorrow, he would have a room prepared for Evelyn, then her sleeping in his bed wouldn't be an issue anymore. Now, he just wanted to rest. Yes, tomorrow he could figure out where Evelyn fit in his life.

"That will be all, Jenkins. Return to your bed. And remember, do not breathe a word of my marriage."

The butler nodded, then opened the adjoining door to Worthington's bedroom and lit the candle near the bed before he left.

Worthington carried Evelyn and laid her on his bed. His wife never moved. She was dead to the world. Her light snores were the only sign that she lived. The past few days had caught up with her, leaving her exhausted. And through their ordeal, she'd never once complained.

Worthington slid her shoes off and went to work on her clothes. He undressed Evelyn, leaving her in a chemise. After he finished, he stripped his own clothes off and collapsed on the bed next to her, his own exhaustion taking hold.

Before he fell asleep, she rolled into him. "Reese?" Evelyn mumbled in her sleep.

"Shh, love. Rest," Worthington mumbled, drawing her into his arms and falling asleep.

~~~~~

A force flung the door open and hopped on the bed, jostling the sleeping occupants. Reese groaned in misery, pulling the covers over his head. However, the interloper ripped them from his hand. He yanked them back before any prying eyes were exposed to his nakedness.

"Wake up, Reese. I want to meet your new bride."

"Maggie, leave him alone. Mother will have your hide. She told us to wait," Noel hissed from the hallway.

"Nonsense. Our brother gets married, then lies in bed all day and we must wait? Most rude." Maggie jumped up and down on the bed to emphasize her point.

The blanket was tugged from Reese's grip again. However, this time, it wasn't his sister trying to grab the blanket. Evelyn was frantically trying to cover herself, a blush spreading across her body. A look of horror rested upon her face. Her wide eyes stared at him in panic, and Reese gave her a devilish grin before pulling Evelyn to his side and lowering his head to kiss her.

"If there is a reason for a delay in my rising, it is because I wish to spend time alone with my bride."

Evelyn tried to squirm out of Reese's hold, which only made him squeeze her tighter. "Reese," she whispered.

"Mmm, I shall allow it since I am about to do this." He lowered his head and kissed his bride good morning.

Once his lips met hers, Evelyn melted. Her embarrassment was forgotten at his gentle kiss. He teased her lips open, and she felt the smile on his face. She enjoyed the teasing nature of her husband, as unexpected as it was. Evelyn relaxed in his hold, losing herself in the kiss. She opened her mouth, drawing Reese in. Their kiss deepened, both forgetting about their audience.

"Oh, how gross," Maggie whined.

Noel sighed from the door. "How romantic."

Reese raised his head, getting lost in Evelyn's eyes. "Get lost, squirt." He lowered his head to return to what promised to be an excellent morning.

That was until his mother's voice rang through the bedroom. "Margaret Ann, remove yourself from your brother's room this instance. Noel, please join Eden in the library for your lesson. Reese, I understand you have news to share with the family. Since over half the day has passed, if you and your bride are fully rested, your family will enjoy hearing the story of how your marriage came to be. I will save your wife any more embarrassment and leave you to your privacy," she ordered before closing the door.

Reese sighed, lowering his head. The spell surrounding them was broken. Evelyn lay tense under him, her face bright red. He rolled off the bed, wrapped a blanket around his waist, and opened the door.

"Jenkins!" he hollered.

Reese didn't have to wait long for the butler to arrive. The servant knew the trouble that lay ahead. Reese had sworn the man to secrecy, but the entire house had discovered the news of his marriage.

"I am sorry, my lord. Murray ran off at the mouth during breakfast to Mrs. Stickler. All the servants heard. Then soon the maids whispered to your mother, sisters, and brother."

"Is the Countess's room prepared?"

Jenkins' head bobbed up and down. "Yes, it is ready for her approval. Mrs. Stickler awaits with Clara, the maid assigned to her, in there now."

ˋ

"And Graham?"

"He returned last week sporting a black eye."

Reese sighed. "Very well. I will show Lady Worthington her suite and introduce her to Mrs. Stickler. Please inform my family that we shall join them for afternoon tea. In the meantime, please send a tray to her lady's room and to mine. We both will require baths."

"Yes, my lord."

Evelyn rose from the bed and wrapped the sheet around herself after Reese dismissed the butler. This wasn't how she imagined meeting her new family for the first time. She didn't remember arriving the previous evening, nor did she remember undressing or sleeping with Reese. The last thing she remembered was watching her husband drink himself into a stupor on the long carriage ride. After growing irritated with his drunken mutterings, she'd closed her eyes. She must have slept deeply to not recall arriving at her husband's estate.

"Umm …" Reese started.

"You have a room to show me." Evelyn didn't want to listen to Reese's explanations. She already saw his shuttered expression, the one he used to keep his distance from her. At this moment, she didn't care. She wanted a few moments to herself before embarking on her new journey. From what she'd just witnessed, she'd left one lively family to join another.

Would her new family grant her the quiet time her own family did? Evelyn had made Uncle Theo a promise to leave her shell behind and experience life to the fullest. What better way than to embrace Reese's family with openness. That way, Reese would have trouble keeping his guard up around her.

Evelyn walked to the door adjoining the two rooms. As with most estates, the bedroom adjoined to the master's was for the lady of the house.

Reese's home would be no different. She waited at the door for him to open it. He held up a finger, then quickly dressed in the clothes he'd worn the day before. He opened the door and ushered Evelyn through. She noted the housekeeper and a maid waiting by the door to the hallway.

"Mrs. Stickler, may I introduce you to my wife, Lady Evelyn Worthington?"

Mrs. Stickler curtsied, offering Evelyn a smile of welcome. "It is a pleasure to welcome you to Worthington Hall, my lady. Let me introduce you to Clara. She will be your lady's maid."

Clara curtsied with less grace. "My lady, it will be my pleasure to serve you," she stuttered.

Evelyn nodded to their greetings. "Thank you for the warm welcome."

Evelyn strolled around the room. She noted how the furniture held a pristine shine. There were fresh flowers on the nightstand and a small fire burning in the grate. The drapes and bedding were worn, the paint was peeling from the walls, and the rug was frayed at the edges.

However, the servants stood proudly to represent the Worthington family. Her husband stood on guard, as if he were waiting for her to object to the room. His pride was on full display.

Evelyn smiled. "The room is lovely. I shall enjoy it immensely."

Mrs. Stickler beamed. She gave orders to Clara to help settle Evelyn in and took her leave, promising to meet with her over the next several days for Evelyn's duties as the new countess. Clara bustled around the bedroom, ordering the footman in to fill the bath, and prepared a plate and tea for Evelyn to eat at the small table near the windows.

"Evelyn?"

Evelyn looked up when Reese spoke her name. Her husband seemed lost on how to handle her. She was lost herself. He took a step toward her and stopped. His mouth opened to speak, then closed again.

Evelyn walked to him and spoke softly, so the servants couldn't hear. "Worthington, I am going to pamper myself with a warm bath and eat a small meal. I suggest you do the same. After we are both feeling like ourselves again, we can talk before we join your family. You have made yourself more than clear on what you require of my wifely duties. However, I am unsure what you wish to tell your family about our marriage. While you are getting ready, I suggest you prepare an explanation, and then you can inform me what I am allowed to say."

Evelyn turned, dismissing him, and joined Clara at the table. She let the maid fuss over her and answered questions pertaining to her care. She glanced out of the corner of her eye to see her husband standing there, dumbfounded by her brush-off.

Evelyn smiled. One point for her.

Reese stared at his wife like a fool. His attempt to show her that he controlled their marriage swung back and hit him square in the face. Evelyn had accepted the bedroom graciously, showed politeness to his servants, and didn't snub her nose at the out-of-date furniture and poor living conditions from what she was used to. Then she calmly informed him how she knew her place as his wife and would accept whatever scheme he wanted to portray to his family. Of course she would. His wife was a devious, manipulative siren. And here he thought she was the meek, biddable twin. What a quandary he was in.

She won that round, but he would win the next.

Chapter Four

Evelyn waited and then waited some more for her husband to inform her on how they were to portray their marriage to his family. However, Reese never came to her bedroom. After a lengthy amount of time, she opened the connecting door to their rooms, only to find his bedroom empty.

She spun on her heel and almost slammed the door in frustration, but decided against it. She wouldn't give the servants a reason to gossip. Where was he?

Evelyn took to pacing back and forth across her room. Her own behavior unsettled her. She had never been one to overreact. However, Reese Worthington brought out emotions in her she never knew she had. For example, she needed to repress her rage at his abandonment. He had no intention of introducing her to his family in a loving manner. Her rage bewildered her. Evelyn's temper used to be gentle, never rising to the situation. Her sister Charlotte was the one to explode without warning, not her. Then there was the matter of turning softhearted at any attention from Reese. He disarmed her defenses. All it took was a kiss and Evelyn melted.

Well, she wouldn't let him deter her from meeting her new family.

While pretending to impersonate Charlotte during the house party, Evelyn had built her confidence. And with that confidence, she would introduce herself to Reese's family.

She pressed her hands down her skirts, calming her nerves. With a swift glance in the mirror to check her appearance, she opened the door and walked right into a lovely young lady. A beauty with flaxen hair and the same eyes as her husband. A dark sapphire gaze too young to be so serious. The girl appeared to hold the weight of the world on her shoulders.

"Please forgive me, I …" Evelyn attempted to apologize.

"You were trying to calm your temper before you made our acquaintance."

"Nonsense."

The girl laughed, and a smile lit her face, making her even more stunning. Evelyn paled in comparison to the beauty before her. "I knocked. You must not have heard me over your pacing."

Evelyn opened her mouth, but nothing came out. She had no excuse.

"I am Eden, Reese's sister. So I am very familiar with how infuriating my brother can be. Mother sent me to gather you two. But, I suppose he is not in his room?"

Evelyn ground her teeth. "No."

Eden gave her a knowing look. "As I said, an infuriating male. Unfortunately, it is a trait the gentlemen in this family hold. I can attempt to make an excuse for him, but it will only be a fib."

"There is no need, Eden. You are not responsible for your brother's ill manners. He is the only one to blame. But as my Aunt Susanna always says, never allow a gentleman to treat you with disrespect. If he does, then make him suffer with kindness." And she intended to do just that. She smiled at her new sister-in-law. "It is a pleasure to meet you, Eden. My name is Evelyn. And for the record, I will not hold Worthington's behavior against you or the rest of your family."

Eden laughed. "You are going to make a wonderful addition to our family." Eden hooked her arm through Evelyn's and guided her along the hallway. "Now come and meet the other heathens."

Eden led Evelyn into the parlor containing the Worthington clan, minus the one who needed to be there. Evelyn gazed upon everyone, taking in their reactions to her appearance. Her protective shell started to rise at their quietness, but it soon lowered once she noticed their smiling faces. Eden patted her hand before she walked away to sit next to her mother on the settee.

The youngest girl jumped out of her seat and came over, dragging Evelyn farther into the parlor. "I told you she was beautiful, Graham," Maggie said to the gentleman leaning against the fireplace mantle.

"I did not refute your claim, Mags. Reese only associates himself with beautiful women. I only stated that Reese's bride must hold some other flaw. Why else would she marry our brother?" The gentleman raised a questioning brow at Evelyn.

The gentleman resembled her husband greatly. From his thick blond waves to his immaculate dress. Like Reese, nothing was out of place. The only difference between the two brothers was this brother exuded charm, from the sparkle in his eyes to the smile hovering on his lips. Oh, if Evelyn weren't so much in love with his infuriating brother, she could have easily fallen for this one.

"Indeed, why? A question I keep asking myself more and more with each passing hour." Evelyn raised her own eyebrow back at him.

He gave her a slow smile. "Ah, my new sister, I believe you have a story to tell. In the meantime, allow me to introduce myself. I am your new brother, Graham."

"Please to meet you, Graham. I have never had a brother before."

"I shall enjoy teaching you the many delights of having one."

"Down, Graham. She is your sister. Stop flirting with your brother's bride." Eden laughed.

Graham waved her away. "Flirting. What nonsense. I am only trying to make our new sister feel comfortable since her husband has failed to do so."

"Please forgive my children."

Evelyn turned toward the older woman's voice. Her mother-in-law smiled fondly at her children's antics. Evelyn relaxed when she noticed the lady's welcoming acceptance.

"There is nothing to forgive. Their banter reminds me of home. I am the one who needs to apologize for not introducing myself. I am Evelyn."

The lady smiled warmly. "Yes, my dear, we know. My son informed me that much. The rest he kept quiet on before he took himself off."

"Ree … Ah, Worthington left?"

"Only to the stables, my dear. I am sure he will be along shortly."

"Oh."

Would he? Evelyn didn't believe so. No, Reese meant to avoid the inquisition concerning their marriage. Which left her to explain the need for their quick union. Reese wouldn't give any explanations because the fault lay with her. Did he believe Evelyn wouldn't admit to her betrayal? Since he'd refused to come to her room to devise a plan to approach his family's questions, then he left Evelyn no choice.

Besides her deceit, Evelyn was not one to lie. Her new family deserved to hear the truth from them, not from the gossipmongers. Evelyn wasn't naïve. She knew the first bit of gossip for the upcoming season would be of their trip to Gretna Green. She didn't look, but their pity filled the air. Evelyn raised her head and gifted them with a genuine smile.

"Please sit, Evelyn. We are all eager to welcome you," said Lady Worthington.

Evelyn sat in the chair nearest her mother-in-law and met her new family. Lady Worthington dismissed the servants, and the tea soon turned into an animated affair. The sisters teased Graham, and he returned their fun with his own humorous remarks, occasionally flirting with Evelyn. Their mother smiled at their foolishness, interjecting her own gaiety from time to time. Evelyn laughed along with them, enjoying herself for the first time in days.

"Why the hasty marriage to Gretna Green?" asked Eden.

"Was it love at first sight?" Noel sighed.

"Does he kiss you much?" asked Maggie.

"He is a fool if he does not," Graham murmured lowly. But not low enough, for Evelyn heard.

Warmth spread across Evelyn's cheeks. She glanced at Lady Worthington to see a secretive smile cross her face that she tried covering with her teacup. The turn in conversation caught Evelyn off guard. Since no one had mentioned the marriage, she'd become comfortable enough to think they would wait for Reese to explain it once he joined them. Since her husband hadn't returned, it seemed his family had grown impatient to hear the story.

"Ahh ..." Evelyn stumbled in her explanation.

They fixed their gazes on her, waiting to hear what they imagined was a love story, but it was far from it. They had welcomed her into their warm embrace and made her feel as if she were one of them. Would they think less of her once she explained how she deceived their brother and forced his hand to marry her?

Evelyn tried to delay telling them. "'Tis a long story."

Which only made Reese's family want to hear it more. Evelyn gulped at their eager faces. This wouldn't paint her in a good light.

Nevertheless, it was a story she needed to tell. After she laid herself bare, she would plead for their forgiveness.

"We have all afternoon, sister," Graham encouraged with a wicked smile. Her new brother knew that any marriage in Gretna Green resulted from scandal.

Evelyn licked her lips. "Very well. Before I begin, please allow me to explain I never intended to trap Reese. My actions were of a simpleminded miss, and for that, I hope I can plead for your forgiveness once you hear the truth."

Graham laughed. "Evelyn, my dear, you married Reese. We are the ones who need to seek your forgiveness. However, your story sounds most interesting, and we await to hear the tale."

Evelyn frowned his way. Her new brother already took pleasure at the demise of Reese without even hearing the story. However, she couldn't resist Graham's incorrigible grin. She shook her head at him, returning his foolish smile.

"For me, the story begins last winter. Reese stayed with my family over the Christmas holiday. It started with an, um … a simple kiss under the mistletoe." Evelyn coughed behind her hand.

Noel sighed. "Ahh, it was love at first sight."

"Only on my end." Evelyn twisted her lips, remembering how her husband had confused her with Charlotte.

"Impossible. Reese must have felt the same," Noel argued.

Evelyn shifted in her seat. "Unfortunately, no. He thought he kissed my sister. Which led to a fiasco at the end of my Uncle Theo's house party."

Graham frowned. "Your sister? My brother is a blind fool."

"No, just a confused one. Charlotte and I did not make it easy for him to tell the difference as we played our schemes on him. Only they backfired on us."

Graham didn't look convinced. "Please explain how Reese could have been so fooled to not tell you apart from your sister."

"My sister Charlotte is my identical twin. 'Tis nothing different about us but our personalities. We differ from night and day. Charlie is lighthearted, adventurous, and feisty. Reese described me to be the dullest of all debutantes, one who would never hold his interest. We switched identities and pretended to be the other, not making it easy to tell us apart, unless you were family and knew the difference. Which Reese did not."

"Ah, Reese's charm is something to be desired. Yet, you profess to hold love for him. Are you mad?" asked Eden.

Evelyn laughed. "I think I am."

"Do continue, dear," Lady Worthington said.

"As I explained, Charlotte and I switched places throughout the house party. At times it seemed as if Reese showed interest. However, it was only to pull information from me on how to charm Charlotte." Evelyn looked down at her hands. "I should have been wiser. He never attempted to charm me. However, when I pretended to be Charlotte, there was this undeniable spark between us. I thought Reese felt it too."

"See, I told you," Noel argued.

Evelyn bestowed her with a wistful smile before continuing to explain the week of the house party to her new family. If she worried they would think less of her, she had been wrong. They were as supportive of her as her own family, which was a comforting thought. But would they be after she told them how she'd caught Reese in her web?

She licked her lips. "On the last night, Uncle Theo held a ball. It was my last attempt to make Reese fall in love with me. However, he wouldn't leave my sister's side. He even asked Charlie for the dinner dance. My heart broke when she answered yes."

Their gasps filled the room at her sister's betrayal, which was so far from the truth.

"Charlie only agreed because Jasper Sinclair had distracted her, which is another story itself. Anyway, Charlie only agreed so she could get rid of Reese. He was a thorn in her side and she figured if she agreed, he would leave her alone for a while. And he did. I finally understood that I never held a chance and never would. With great despair, I retired to my bedroom to lick my wounds."

Graham smirked. "I am in love with your sister. Is she available?"

Evelyn laughed. "No, I am afraid not. You would never have had any luck with her anyhow."

"Jasper Sinclair?"

"Yes."

Graham tsked. "The lucky blighter. Oh, well, you win some, you lose some."

"I still adore her, and we have not even met her yet," said Eden.

Lady Worthington shot her children a look. "Children, you are being unfair toward your brother. What will Evelyn think of us?"

Graham snorted. "Mother, I think our dear new sister has the gist of her husband's character. There is no need for us to put on empty airs around her. Evelyn will learn soon enough the full depth of his character and she needs to know she has our support."

Evelyn bit her lip. "You may not feel the same way after I finish my story."

Eden smiled brightly at her. "Nonsense."

Evelyn took a deep breath and continued. "As I lay crying on my bed, Charlie arrived in our bedroom. When she noticed my tears, she comforted me and explained her reasons for accepting Reese's invitation. I knew she never meant to betray me. Her heart was as confused as mine. Our cousin Lucas arrived for Charlie. Her horse had gone into labor, and they needed her help. Charlie changed her clothes and promised to plan a new strategy on her return. However, I took matters into my own hands. I saw her discarded dress and took it upon myself to change into it. I brushed out my hair as Charlie had hers styled and I returned to the ball to wait for Reese to claim Charlie's hand for the dinner dance."

Evelyn paused, unsure how to continue. The room held an eerie silence. She hazarded a glance around the room to catch their reactions. They appeared eager to hear the rest, Reese's mother and brother already drawing their own conclusions. "The rest is history."

"Your story is far from over. You have left out the most scandalous of details," baited Graham.

Evelyn cast a glance at Margaret. "Yes, well, those details are not for the ears of innocence. The rest you can assume and would probably be correct."

Graham sighed. "You have a point, my dear. Anyway, it ended by giving us a new sister to call our own."

Lady Worthington drummed her fingers on the arm of her seat. "Graham, perhaps, you and Margaret can find your brother and inform him he missed tea, but I will not tolerate him missing dinner."

Graham nodded his understanding. His mother wished to hear the full details of Reese's journey to the marriage alter, details that weren't suitable for Maggie. He would love to hear the rest of the story, but already understood what happened. Graham knew Reese attended the house party to gain a wife, however he married the wrong twin. At least with this scandal hanging over their family's head, Graham's antics would go unnoticed.

"Come along, Mags, I believe we will find Reese in the stables." Graham walked over to his new sister, lifted her hand, and placed a kiss upon her knuckles. With a wink, he and Maggie left the parlor.

"You may continue, my dear." Lady Worthington sat back on the settee with her hands clasped in front of her.

Evelyn hesitated. "It is most inappropriate for Eden and Noel to hear."

Lady Worthington shook her head. "No, they must understand how even a gentleman can act. Brother or not, Reese displayed the behavior of a scoundrel. Not the gentleman I raised him to be. I taught him how to treat a lady as a precious gift. I am afraid Reese has taken the character of my late husband lately. I prayed that day would never happen. However, his actions speak otherwise."

The only option Evelyn held was to continue her story. Her mother-in-law had a point. Before long, she would launch her daughters in the Marriage Mart and they needed to prepare themselves against unscrupulous gentlemen. Not that Reese was unscrupulous. Evelyn held that trait. Still, he took her innocence, and for that, it made him guilty. Even though she had given herself to Reese willingly.

"Very well." Evelyn inclined her head. "When the dinner dance started, Reese claimed the dance. Once again, while he held me in his arms, the sparks ignited and only built the longer we were in each other's company. During dinner, he sequestered an intimate table for two. We talked little, just stared into each other's eyes with the unspoken question of whether to act upon our desire. With each touch of affection, I knew what I wanted. And that was him. I held no doubt of the feelings I held for Reese. At that point, I no longer cared if he did not realize who I was."

Lady Worthington sighed. "It should have mattered, Evelyn."

"I see that now. At the time, it only mattered that he desired me, too."

Noel pursed her lips. "I do not care that nobody believes me, but I think that Reese cares for you too. Did he share the same spark with Charlotte?"

Evelyn shook her head. "No, I do not believe he did."

Triumph gleamed in Noel's eyes. "There, you see. He may have been blind, but his heart knew the difference."

"I wish that were true."

"What happened after dinner?" asked Eden.

"We stepped out onto the terrace for a breath of fresh air. After the other guests entered the ballroom, Reese pulled us into a darkened corner and kissed me." Evelyn sighed.

Noel sighed, too. While she knew Noel believed it all to be romantic, Evelyn wished it had been all directed toward her, not Charlotte.

"Then?" Eden prompted.

"One thing led to another, and we ended the ball spent in each other's arms in his bedroom."

"May I ask why?" asked Lady Worthington.

Evelyn blushed, her face on fire from the direct question. How could she explain the reasons to Reese's mother on what tempted her to throw caution to the wind? How did one explain how the fire Reese ignited in her turned into a passionate frenzy? That, even now, if he were to come into the parlor and crook his finger her way, she would follow him anywhere he desired.

"Honestly?"

Lady Worthington cocked an eyebrow. "Yes."

"I do not understand myself. It is as I explained to my sister. Reese makes me feel alive. He gives me a reason to live. For years, I lived inside a shell after I lost my parents, too afraid of life. After one kiss from Reese, the fear I clung to vanished. When he arrived at the house party, I wanted to explore those feelings to see if I imagined them. And I did not. The connection held strong, tempting me to explore the depths of its bond."

Lady Worthington wanted to sigh at Evelyn's description of her son's unorthodox attempt of courtship. The blush across Evelyn's cheeks only accented her beauty. Her son was a fool, just as his father had been. She wholeheartedly approved of the union. The new countess would elevate their family in society once again. Evelyn was polite, graceful, and held a kindness in her eyes that was illuminated with each word she spoke. No mother wanted their child to marry in haste. For Reese to take that risk only proved he harbored feelings for the girl, ones he would no doubt deny because of Evelyn's deception. The entire family needed to make Reese see reason. And reason he would see. If not, then he would lose the most amazing gift he received.

Evelyn wouldn't stay and endure heartache the way she had. Lady Worthington had loved her foolhardy husband just as passionately. However, he had never felt the same. If he had, he never would have strayed. He'd returned to his bachelor ways after securing enough children to keep her occupied and out of his business. Nay, his life. She would use everything in her power to make sure her son didn't make the same mistake. Their passionate embrace this morning hadn't gone unnoticed. She wasn't mistaken. The spark sizzled in the air surrounding them.

"I understand. Now, girls, let this be a lesson to you. A true gentleman would secure your happiness before his own. If any gentleman persuades you to be alone with him, it is only because of nefarious reasons. Not all will end with him taking your hand in marriage. Your brother may have demonstrated the behavior of a scoundrel, but in the end, he was a gentleman and married Evelyn. Not all of them will."

"Yes, Mother," Eden and Noel answered.

"Now that we understand the complete story and depths of Evelyn's emotions toward Reese, we will now help Evelyn to win Reese's heart," Lady Worthington said and winked at Evelyn.

Chapter Five

Worthington stood with one arm on the top rail of the fence and one booted foot resting on a lower rung. He watched his trainer exercise Mayhem. The horse was his latest acquisition before his father died and left him without the finances to see to the horse's success.

Still, he made sure the horse kept trained to race. One day, he would have the funds to enter him at Newmarket. He had a month to shift his funds around before the horserace. If Mayhem won, he stood a chance at making a small fortune from the winnings.

He tried to enjoy the training, but his guilty conscience kept nagging at him on what a bastard he was by abandoning Evelyn to deal with his family alone. Hell, knowing his family, they had already taken her side. Everything he did lately, they found fault with. Eden most of all. His mother had made plans for Eden to make her debut this season, but with the family's limited funds, he had to nix the plan. The cost of new dresses made him shudder.

"I thought this might be where you hauled your tail to hide," drawled Graham.

Maggie jumped on the fence next to him, hanging on the top rail with her feet dangling below. She held her gaze fastened on Mayhem.

"Evelyn is smashing, Reese. We all agree that she makes the perfect addition to our family, even though you ruined her with a kiss. I think there was more, but Mama made me leave."

If only a simple kiss ruined Evelyn Holbrooke. No, it involved more than a kiss. It was an evening he kept reliving over and over whenever he closed his eyes.

Had Evelyn shared the details of their horrid courtship with his family? No, she wouldn't. They had agreed to discuss what his family should know… However, he'd given away that option by not joining her in her bedroom and staying away from tea, hadn't he? The temptation to be alone with her was too strong. If Worthington joined his family for tea, he could have directed the conversation as he saw fit. Now he would have to deal with the aftermath of her confession.

It couldn't be too bad since the chit was too shy to share such intimate details. He didn't think her dull for no reason at all. He'd given her many opportunities to interact with him during the house party. Instead, Evelyn had clammed up. Her shyness caused her to stutter when nervous. He wondered how she had captured his attention as Charlotte. Perhaps they never switched places. Did they play Sinclair and him for fools? Did Charlotte dally with both men and chose Sinclair the victor? Either way, Evelyn was now the wife he was saddled with.

Then he recalled their wedding night. The girl he slept with was no virgin. Was that the reason for their deception? Did another gentleman pass her over, and they used him to secure Evelyn a marriage with a peer? He sighed. Foolish wonderings. That was all they were. Worthington didn't believe them himself. Evelyn had been a virgin the night he made love to her. She was the twin who had gotten under his skin and captured a part of him. He clung to the remaining part of his soul, for fear of the power Evelyn would hold over him if he allowed her too close. A power he would never relinquish.

"What I do not understand is how you could ever mistake the lovely Evelyn with anyone else?" baited Graham.

Worthington raised his eyebrows. "You realize her sister is her identical twin."

Graham waved his hand. "Rubbish. They may look alike, but they sound like two different ladies. How could you not tell the difference? Charlotte must be a wild hellion. I do not need to explain to you how amazing Evelyn is. Divine would be too tame of a description."

Worthington growled at his brother's regard toward his bride. He must make sure they were never left alone. His brother held no set of boundaries. Graham's indulgence of the opposite sex put most gentlemen to shame, including himself.

By then the trainer walked by, urging Maggie to help him brush down Mayhem. With a jump over the fence, his younger sister skipped alongside Mayhem, chattering with the trainer.

Now that Maggie was gone, Reese pierced Graham with his stare. "I will only say this once. You are to keep your distance from Evelyn."

Graham met his gaze defiantly. "Why, big brother? Do you consider me competition? That's nonsense since you already won her hand. I consider Evelyn to be a very dear sister that I shall enjoy growing close to on a friendly basis."

Worthington advanced on Graham, then backed off when he noticed Graham took pleasure in baiting him. He had done that their entire lives. His brother took nothing and no one serious. So, getting angry at his brother would solve nothing. Plus, Worthington couldn't afford to allow his family to understand the power Evelyn held over him. If any of them learned, they wouldn't hesitate to conspire with Evelyn.

"What has my wife shared of our courtship?" asked Worthington.

"Enough to know that your so-called marriage was a hasty union. It would appear you ruined *our* lovely Evelyn in the most scandalous of settings. As a guest of her uncle's no less." Graham made a tsking sound.

Reese ground his teeth. "Did *my* lovely Evelyn explain her deception in trapping me?"

"I only had the pleasure of learning a small portion of her deception. Mother dismissed Maggie and I from the parlor before allowing Evelyn to finish her story. I shall have to learn the details from Eden later."

Worthington moaned. He didn't think his wife was capable of sharing her guilt about their marriage. But it would appear he'd underestimated her. Now his entire family knew of the sordid debacle. He felt his mother's disapproval all ready. Oh, not at Evelyn. His mother would lay the blame at his feet.

With his thoughts wrapped up in Evelyn, Worthington didn't take notice when Graham changed the conversation. His brother inquired about Mayhem's entry in Newmarket.

Reese shook his head. "No, I have no available funds. I still need to raise the money for the entry fee."

"That should be no problem once you receive Evelyn's dowry. She should have a nice settlement since she is one of the Duke of Colebourne's wards."

"Which I tried to negotiate when I thought I had slept with Charlotte. The duke refused any agreement until I married Evelyn. We did not part on the best of circumstances, so I do not expect a generous offering coming in my direction."

Graham chuckled lowly. "Yes, I can understand calling the duke's niece a dull debutante would not please Colebourne. I did not imagine you for a dimwit, brother."

"Not one of my finer moments."

Graham glanced at him out of the corner of his eye. "Is that your true opinion of Evelyn?"

Worthington sighed. "No."

Worthington refused to discuss the matter of Evelyn. Graham would just have to wonder how he felt about his bride. Worthington had yet to examine his feelings, for he feared Evelyn meant more to him than he wanted her to.

Graham nodded in understanding. "Mother demands your presence at dinner since you missed tea. I am to issue her threat if you do not concede."

Of course she did. "I will be at dinner. In fact, I think I will interrupt their tea now. Will you make sure Mags keeps out of their way inside the stables?"

"Will do." Graham smiled, watching Reese's quick strides toward the house. He'd baited his brother with enough information to make him wonder what Evelyn had said. He was correct. His return home would go unnoticed in place of Reese's nuptials. Graham whistled, walking into the stables in search of Maggie.

~~~~~

Worthington lurked outside the parlor doors, listening to Evelyn laugh with his mother and sisters. The soft melodic sound settled over him, conjuring memories of their time spent alone.

He banged his head back on the wall, calling himself a fool. The signs were there all along, but the prize had blinded him toward their duplicity. While Evelyn's laughter was a melody that soothed his soul, Charlotte's laughter had confused him. It left him feeling empty. He hadn't understood the chit's sense of humor and how it kept changing. Now he saw the differences. Did Evelyn laugh at him now? Did she find humor in her deception? How she must have laughed with her family over his ignorance. And now with his family.

He stepped in the doorway and waited for their attention. However, they paid him no heed. Instead, they fell into another peal of laughter. Evelyn laughed so hard, tears slipped from her eyes. She wiped them away, laughing harder. All at his expense.

He cleared his throat, capturing their attention. But not the attention he wanted. His mother's disapproving stare said everything. Even though he was the head of the family, it still didn't keep him from falling under his mother's wrath. He would deal with her later. Now he wanted to address his wife and her chatter of their courtship. He needed to end this now before he became more fodder for his sibling's entertainment.

"Lady Worthington, I expect you in my study at once." With that, Worthington turned and stomped away.

Eden laughed. "Oh, my, Reese is in a snit. Which Lady Worthington do you imagine he wishes to scold?"

Lady Worthington sighed. "Girls, please allow me a moment with Evelyn before she has to meet with Reese."

"Yes, Mama," replied Eden and Noel.

After Reese's sisters left, Lady Worthington grabbed Evelyn's hand.

"I do not know the direction to his study."

It was a pointless comment to make. There were many servants who could direct her to Reese. His anger vibrated with his order. And she knew why. They'd found humor at his expense. When Reese's family opened their arms so generously toward her, Evelyn had relaxed in their company, enjoying how they bantered with each other. It reminded Evelyn of her own family.

"I will show you. I need to speak with you while we have a moment alone." Lady Worthington stood.

Evelyn nodded. "That would be lovely."

Lady Worthington motioned for her, and Evelyn fell into step beside her. "I believe you will be good for Reese. Do not allow his bark to cower you. He has not always been so brisk. At one time, he joined in with our tomfoolery. However, after his father left our family in dire straits, he lost his sense of humor, and I am afraid he is showing his father's temperament. Now with his breeding program on the brink of failure, he lets his frustration rule his actions."

"That explains his reason for accepting Uncle Theo's bet."

Lady Worthington glanced at her curiously. "What bet?"

Evelyn waved it away. "It is a long story. The short version is that Uncle Theo baited the gentlemen at the house party. Whoever won Charlotte's hand would get the foal of a horse in his stable. He only goaded the gentlemen because one of them had already ruined Charlotte and he wanted that man to step forward. Instead, it caused a catastrophic confusion. That is why Worthington pursued Charlotte. And because of our deception, he lost what would have helped him financially. What a mess I have created."

"Was it?"

Evelyn looked down. "Yes."

Lady Worthington hummed. "I disagree. You are what my son needs. Not a horse. Not financial gain. Only you."

Evelyn wished that were true. "I do not see how."

Lady Worthington smiled. "Because you, my dear, will create a family with Reese and give him a sense of stability that he has always craved. He does not understand what he needs, but he will."

"I hope you are correct."

"Trust me. I am. Now, shall we deliver you to the dungeon?" Lady Worthington laughed at her own pun.

Evelyn laughed along with her. "Lead me away."

Lady Worthington led Evelyn along the hallway toward Reese's study. She pointed out different rooms and told Evelyn she would give her a tour tomorrow. Once they reached the formidable room, Lady Worthington wrapped Evelyn in a motherly hug. The comforting gesture reminded Evelyn of her own mother. Over the years, her older sister Jacqueline and Aunt Susanna had hugged her when she needed the support of a loved one, but their affection never measured up to the tender embrace of a mother. A gesture that wiped away your troubles and warmed your heart.

When tears came to her eyes, Evelyn realized she had missed her mother more than she thought. She clung to Reese's mother for a moment and then pulled away before she embarrassed herself. When she drew away, Lady Worthington tilted her head at the door and smiled her support before she walked away.

Since there were no footmen near the door to announce her arrival, Evelyn took it upon herself to knock and wait for permission to enter. She didn't have to wait long before Reese threw the door open. Her husband stood in the open frame, glaring at her. Evelyn tried to hold on to her confidence, but some of it withered away under Reese's fury. She had never had to deal with an angry male. Her uncle and cousin had never raised their voices at any of their mishaps. They only pointed out their mistakes so they could learn from them. While Reese had shown signs of his fury since they left Uncle Theo's estate, it was nothing compared to the state he was in now.

There was a trace of hurt in his regard. Before she searched his gaze for more, his eyes shuttered, shutting himself off from Evelyn getting too close. It would appear there were many facets to her new husband. Evelyn had allowed lust to blind her into believing what they shared was love. She needed to discover the layers that made Reese the man he was today. But would he allow Evelyn to learn who that person was?

"Finally, madam. I am so glad that you replied to your summons with such haste." His words dripped with sarcasm. "Perhaps next time you might consider my valuable time does not revolve around your schedule, but mine."

Evelyn sighed, drawing on Lady Worthington's advice. In the past, she had apologized to put another at ease. However, she was no longer that Evelyn. Nor would she allow Reese to intimidate her. He thought her the meek and mild twin, too afraid to speak for herself. Well, she would show him that he didn't know her so well, either.

Evelyn drew herself up. "Your mother requested a private word. I paid her the respect I knew you would expect of me and granted her the time she requested."

Reese paused before he continued his tirade. He hadn't been expecting Evelyn to respond with an excuse. He searched her gaze for any deception, but only truth shone from those depths. Depths of emerald gems glistening with hope. He couldn't allow hope into his life. Hope wouldn't secure him the funds he needed.

He ushered Evelyn inside the room and closed the doors from any outside lurkers. He knew his family would listen through the doors. If he could keep their voices down, they would be none the wiser on his anger toward Evelyn. He led her to the chair in front of his desk. Then he moved to sit behind the enormous, over-the-top creation his father had designed to showcase wealth he never held. The only promising thing about the monstrosity was the distance it kept between him and his wife.

Just holding Evelyn's elbow for a few seconds had enflamed his senses. Her scent of raspberries and vanilla wafted in the air. He closed his eyes, the fragrance reminding him of stolen kisses in a linen closet. Her soft moans at his caress undid him then, as they did now. Then Reese remembered another time he tried to steal a kiss and was slapped for his attempt. That time the scent of chocolate biscuits surrounded her. Charlotte. Another sign.

How would Evelyn taste now? Would the flavor of lemons explode on his tongue from the lemon cake he noticed sitting on the tray in the parlor? Or perhaps she tasted of pure sugar? He noticed how she took her tea, more sugar than the liquid itself. If he stroked his tongue along hers, would she sigh into his kiss?

"You wished to speak with me." Evelyn's voice penetrated his musings.

Reese shook his head to clear his thoughts. Why did he become so distracted in her mere presence?

"Yes. I did not give you permission to tell my family of the reason for our marriage. I specifically told you we would discuss what to present to them. My younger sisters should not have heard the sordid details. You, madam, had no right."

She met his gaze directly. "I apologize if I have offended their innocent ears. If you recall, you were to come to my bedroom to discuss what we would share. Instead, you slinked away and left me to face your family on my own."

Reese sat up straighter in his chair, puffing out his chest. "I did not slink away. I had matters to see to. You were to wait in your room until I came for you."

She cocked an eyebrow. "But you never arrived, nor did you have any inclination to. Your mother sent Eden to collect me. Once I met your family, I decided I would not play them false with stories that held no truth."

He gnashed his teeth together. "So, you will not lie to my family, but I am an exception? Your conscience did not seem to have a problem when your every action toward me has been a lie."

Evelyn cringed at his tone. He never intended for them to move past her deception. She held no clue how to correct her mistakes. Only time would heal the wounds she'd caused. "I see your family no different from mine. They know the truth of my actions, and I felt your family should, too. If they did not hear the truth from us, the gossip mill would take pleasure in informing them of our misdeed."

"It was not your place to tell," Reese snarled, rising to his feet.

Evelyn clenched her hands in her lap. "What is my place then, *Lord Worthington*?"

His eyes flashed in anger. "Your place is to stay silent. To be invisible. If I recall, that should not be so difficult for you to achieve. After all, you are the dull ward to the Duke of Colebourne. The girl who blended into the shadows that no one ever heard a peep from. That is what I require from you in my home. I do not want to notice you ever in my presence. I understand that we must share meals with my family. Those are the only instances you are to be within my vision. How you spend your days is of no consequence to me. Do not waste my time on any of your needs. My mother will be of assistance should you require anything. Are we clear, *Lady Worthington*?"

Evelyn rose, lifting her chin with what pride she had remaining. "Very clear."

She walked to the door. When he spoke, her hand stilled on the doorknob.

"And, Evelyn, please make sure you send a missive to your uncle about our marriage nuptials. I expect a sizable reward for providing you with my name."

If Reese's demands for keeping away from him weren't clear on his feelings toward her, his last remark settled with misery in her gut. Evelyn didn't reply to his last request. She opened the door and walked smack dab into Graham. He wrapped his arms around her to steady her. She lifted her tear-filled gaze to his and saw pity. With a gasp, she untangled herself and walked away swiftly.

Graham stood in the doorway, shaking his head at Reese. "Was that necessary?"

Reese clenched his teeth. "She needed to understand her position as my wife. Her uncle coddled Evelyn her entire life. I do not have the patience. Nor do I care for her in the same regard to continue where the duke left off. No, it is best she learn her place in my life."

"The way mother learned her place in father's life?"

"Exactly," Reese replied, but not with the same emphasis as his earlier statements.

Graham's eyes roamed over Reese with distaste. "Mmm, yes. I can see you are shaping up to be a replica of our sire. Even down to the cruel treatment of your wife. He would have been proud. Now Mother, she will be sorely disappointed to hear how you treat Evelyn. Such a shame. Since you have no need for your wife's companionship, then you will not mind if I seek her company for idle conversation and such."

Reese advanced on Graham so fast, neither of them realized how deeply Graham provoked Reese.

"You keep your philandering ways clear of *my* wife," Reese snarled in Graham's face.

However, Graham only smiled at Reese's temper. It would appear his brother protested too much where Evelyn was concerned. Reese may say he wanted no interaction with Evelyn, only when necessary, but Graham saw the effect Evelyn held over Reese. His brother was smitten and didn't even realize it. It was only Graham's brotherly duty toward Evelyn that kept provoking Reese to confront his feelings for the sweet girl.

Graham didn't back down. "I only wish to offer *my* new sister brotherly companionship."

"I will not repeat myself again. Stay away from *my* wife."

Graham cocked an eyebrow. "Or else?"

"Or I will cut your allowance off. You will not receive another coin from the estate."

Graham shrugged his indifference to Reese's threat. He continued to let Reese believe he needed his allowance to survive. When, in fact, he didn't. Graham had his own source of income that his family wasn't privy to. And he would continue to keep it from them. For now. He refused to risk their lives by giving them the knowledge of his wealth. To them, he would remain the penniless, troublemaking, spendthrift rake they and the ton believed him to be.

Reese watched his brother walk away moments after his wife departed. Both conversations left him feeling drained. He poured himself a glass of brandy, drained it in one swallow, and then poured himself another. He wandered back to sit behind the desk, running his hand across the top. Was there any truth in Graham's comment? Was he turning into his father? He shuddered at the thought. Yet, his behavior today alone showed signs of his father's character.

Reese thought he was better than his elder. However, his demands to Evelyn spoke otherwise. Still, he wouldn't bend. Evelyn needed to learn her place in his life and deal with the consequences of her actions. Just because he married her didn't mean he forgave her for her deception. In time, he would relent on his restrictions. But for now, Reese's sanity needed Evelyn kept at a distance.

Chapter Six

Reese sat surrounded around the dinner table with his family in silence. The conversation that flowed around him was subdued, the familiar humor no longer displayed. It had changed the day he ordered his wife to stay invisible. For a month his family's polite indifference held strong. They made their position clear. They pledged their allegiance with Evelyn. Graham had spread Reese's orders to his mother and sisters. His mother's wrath still lingered over his disregard toward Evelyn.

Reese's gaze trailed to the end of the table. Evelyn's seat sat empty at every dinner. Reese could count on one hand the instances he came across her. On those encounters, she acknowledged him, then made herself scarce. It was what he wanted. Then why did he feel out of sorts, as if a part of him were missing?

He discovered that she took her breakfast in his mother's suite every morning at eight. Reese spent his days filled with appointments, calls on his tenants, or working with the horses so he never joined them for luncheon. But Evelyn did. Sometimes he walked by the dining room to listen to her talk and soak in her laughter. Reese never joined them because he meant to stand firmly by his decision. He wasn't so cruel though to deny her the companionship of his family. And every evening she took a tray in her room, never once offering an excuse. They each shared the enjoyment of his family on their own.

However, Evelyn's presence was everywhere in his home. Her scent wafted in the air, her laughter filled the rooms, and her influence on his family was apparent. Everyone went out of their way to welcome Evelyn into their family and to Worthington Hall. Everyone but him.

Though, in the dark of night, he regretted his stand. Reese overheard Evelyn humming softly in her bedroom and wished to be in her company. He wanted to twist the doorknob and open the door that kept them separated. But he never did. Instead, he held his palms against the grain, wanting the pull of their connection to reach Evelyn. Reese ached to hold her in his arms again, to kiss her soft lips, and to caress her silken limbs. Would she refuse him if he were to open the door?

Reese's gaze continued to travel around the table, taking in each member of his family. He noticed the subtle changes since Evelyn's arrival and knew her influence over them was the reason. His family talked among themselves quietly, not wanting to set him off. Since his return home, he had taken his frustration out on them. Though they weren't at fault, their consideration toward Evelyn over him hurt deeply.

His latest turn of bad luck had been this afternoon after the post arrived. It was worse than he would ever let his family know. The Duke of Colebourne had responded to Evelyn's letter. It wasn't in his favor. The duke requested a visit once they reached London, to see for himself how his niece fared. Reese didn't have any intention of taking Evelyn to London for the season. There was no need since they had already wed. There was the matter of their depleted funds. He'd already cancelled Eden's debut and refused to cause a rift by taking Evelyn to town. Reese would have to swallow his pride and plead his case to the duke. Perhaps during his trip to London, the duke would allow him an appointment.

Yes, that was the answer. Also, he needed a reason to leave. The farther away from Evelyn, the better chance he had of regaining his sanity.

He would visit his old haunts and check out Tattersalls. He also had two calls he needed to make since he'd tied the knot. He regretted that he would have to hurt his mistresses, but a promise was a promise. Even if only to oneself. Reese held onto his anger, but he would never hurt Evelyn in that matter. Once he returned, he would inform Evelyn that he would visit her bed nightly until she conceived. He needed an heir. Reese couldn't count on his irresponsible brother to take care of their family.

"That sounds like a fabulous idea, Noel!" Reese heard his mother exclaim.

"What is?" Reese asked.

Silence settled over the table. His family suddenly found interest in their plates. Reese didn't know roasted hen and vegetables were so entertaining.

"Noel?"

"I thought we might take a picnic by the pond tomorrow. Evelyn has yet to explore the grounds," Noel answered while staring at their mother.

The mention of Evelyn hung in the air. They thought he paid no attention to their conversations. He tried not to, but every time they mentioned his wife's name, his ears perked up, wanting to hear more.

"I agree with Mother. It is an excellent idea."

"It is?" Noel squeaked. Her eyes shifted around to gauge everyone's reaction.

"Yes. I shall inform Evelyn of the entertainment while you organize the picnic details with Eden and Mother. Graham, you will see to the traveling conveyances. Mags, your job is to gather food for the ducklings." Reese stood. "Now if you will pardon me, I have paperwork to finish."

With a fresh spring to his step, Reese headed to his study. He would appear busy for the next few hours. Then before bed, he would knock on

Evelyn's door. After he informed Evelyn of the plans for tomorrow, he would attempt his seduction. Why wait for his return from London to trick her with his devotion? He would begin tonight.

"Should we warn Evelyn that Reese is going to talk to her?" asked Eden.

Lady Worthington glanced at her daughter. "No. We must not give cause to Reese's temper. Her absence from dinner is bothering him. Perhaps he wishes to turn a new leaf with Evelyn. We shall wait and see how the picnic progresses tomorrow. If he still hasn't changed, we shall move to Plan B."

"Which is?" asked Graham.

"That, my boy, is where you will come in."

A wicked smile spread across Graham's face. He understood his mother's intention and knew Reese would fall for the bait. They had competed their entire life. Evelyn would be no exception. Graham didn't want Evelyn for himself. He wanted his brother to see the happiness that lay before him. And if flirting with Evelyn helped to achieve that outcome, then he was game. He only hoped he wouldn't have to use Evelyn as a pawn.

"It will be my pleasure."

~~~~~~

Evelyn curled up on the divan and stared into the darkness. This used to be her favorite part of the day, a time to reflect on her thoughts and to lose herself in a book. She used to love having time to herself. Now she dreaded it. Since marrying Reese, it had become a time of isolation. Not that she never left her room. Her days were full by spending time with his family. They were enjoyable and helped to ease her homesickness.

While his family adored him, they also knew his faults to a tee. They offered her support and guidance, begging for her patience on his disgruntled attitude. Reese's mother pleaded for Evelyn to give him a chance. His sisters varied from plotting his demise for his boorish behavior to telling her stories of when he was their hero. Then there was Graham. She couldn't wish for a more fitting brother. He offered her a companionship filled with friendly overtures. He never spoke a degrading word toward his brother. Evelyn noticed Graham admired Reese and his accomplishments for their family. Whenever Evelyn appeared melancholy, Graham charmed Evelyn into a smile. Before long, he would have her giggling over his silly attempts at humor.

As she ate dinner alone, she reflected on Reese's order. While it appeared that she had cowered under his words, it was far from the truth. She'd obliged by his wishes, making herself scarce from him. But she had only done so to allow Reese time to adjust to her presence in his home. To allow his anger time to simmer.

On the few times they had encountered each other, she'd acknowledged him and then removed herself. Only those moments didn't happen by accident. Evelyn was aware of Reese whenever he was in the house. The pull of their attraction always alerted her to when he was near. His deep voice rang through the air, and his scent lingered in the hallways. She would follow those clues to find him. Anything for a glimpse of him. Before he noticed, Evelyn would drink him in. Absorb all that was Reese.

Would he ever forgive her? Or was this the precedent for their marriage?

Every night she lay in bed, hoping the adjoining door would open and Reese would stroll through demanding his husbandly rights. Not that he would have to demand. She would welcome him into her arms. Mind you, she wasn't a weak-willed woman who allowed a man to control her. She was a woman who loved her husband and wanted him to return her love.

Evelyn believed they could overcome her deceit and build a firm foundation for the years to come. To do so, she needed to give Reese the time he needed.

It had been a month now. Whenever she came upon him, he no longer snarled in her direction. Over the last week, his family had informed her Reese had started inquiring about Evelyn's comfort or her whereabouts. She felt in her heart that Reese was warming up to her. She hoped to have his forgiveness soon.

A knock sounded on the door, startling Evelyn from her musings. Before she replied, the door between their bedrooms opened, and Reese strolled inside. His sudden appearance froze Evelyn in her seat. She devoured him with her eyes, taking in his casual attire. He'd discarded his cravat, suit coat, and waistcoat. He undid the buttons on his shirt, displaying his firm chest.

Evelyn's fingers itched to caress the warm skin. She curled her hand into a fist to stop herself from rising and acting on her fantasies. Reese's tawny locks stood on ends, as if he had run his fingers through his hair multiple times. Evelyn's gaze continued to trail his form, and her eyes locked onto the front of his trousers.

It would appear she wasn't the only one excited to see the other.

Reese coughed, drawing Evelyn out of her perusal. Her cheeks warmed, which wasn't the only part of her body on fire from Reese. She started to rise when he held out an arm to stop her progress.

"Please, stay relaxed."

Evelyn lowered herself back against the cushions. But relax? No. As long as Reese stood so near, her body would remain tense. The only way she could relax was if he drew her into his arms. Since his actions showed no signs of affection, Evelyn would remain coiled, ready to spring.

"How are you?"

"How am I?" Evelyn squeaked.

His lips twisted into a slight grin, and a sparkle brightened his eyes. Was he playing with her? Or did he genuinely care for her comfort? "Yes. Are you settling into your new home? Has my family made you feel welcomed?"

She licked her lips. "Yes. Your family is a delight, and your home is very comforting. It reminds me of home. I have even started taking over some duties from your mother."

"Excellent. This is your home now, Evelyn. The servants should seek your guidance for decisions concerning the house. Please, make any changes as you see fit."

"I will."

Reese nodded, taking in Evelyn stretched out on the divan. Her hair flowed against the light cushions, emphasizing the dark strands. A book lay nestled in her lap. Reese knew it to be her favorite pastime. Whenever he visited the Colebourne estate, he'd noticed Evelyn with her nose in a book, quiet as a mouse. Another sign he let past. He never once saw Charlotte reading. It was Evelyn who came into the Colebourne's library at Christmas. Even when he seduced her, she was quiet. The only sound coming from her lips were the sweetest moans of pleasure. If he kissed her now, would she respond with those same sweet moans? Or would she object with her displeasure at his behavior since they arrived?

"Did you require something, Worthington?"

Did he require something? Yes, Reese required a great deal from his wife. But he knew his cruel behavior would prevent him from receiving her gentle touch. Her sweet lips under his. Her body molded around his, moving as one. Oh, he required more than he realized.

"You have been absent from dinner since your arrival."

Evelyn stiffened. He had the audacity to comment on her absence when he had made his position very clear. She had only followed his instructions to stay invisible from his sight. She thought she had followed Reese's orders to perfection. Now he wished to discuss her absence as if there were another reason but his own command. At this rate, she wouldn't ever understand her husband.

She met his stare boldly.

"You made my position in your household clear. I am only following your instructions."

He held his hands together behind his back and walked farther into the room. "I never forbade you from joining our family for dinner."

"My days are filled with your family. I stayed away to allow you time with them. So you may enjoy them without tension filling the air. They should not have their life ruined by our disagreements."

He nodded. "I agree, my lady. Hopefully, we can put that aside. I hope you will join our family for a picnic on the morrow. You have my promise that I will leave my disgruntled mood behind."

She didn't answer immediately. "No, I shall remain in my room. I hope you can find enjoyment with your family. It sounds like it will be a joyous afternoon."

"You must come. Mags is gathering the food for the ducklings."

She perked up at that. "You have ducklings?"

Reese hid a smile at her question. Evelyn might have been skittish around horses, but he noticed her care toward the other animals on his estate. When he followed her and Mags to the stable yesterday, he spied Evelyn cooing over the baby kittens. Her hand stroked the soft fur with a gentleness he remembered oh so well.

"Yes, too many to count."

She bit her lip, torn. "Mmm."

"Would you like to see them?"

She nodded reluctantly. "Yes."

Evelyn realized Reese's trick. But why? What was his motive to have her join his family for a picnic tomorrow? Why the shift in his acceptance of her presence in his home? Was it because of her uncle's reply? Uncle Theo had responded to her marital announcement with relief that Reese saw to her welfare. He wrote of his pleasure that Evelyn had settled in comfortably at Worthington Hall and that Reese's family had welcomed her with open arms. However, her uncle didn't believe Reese's regard toward Evelyn.

Uncle Theo remained unconvinced, especially since Evelyn had never once mentioned Reese or the nature of their marriage in her letters. And for that, her uncle refused to gift them with a marriage settlement. No, Uncle Theo held the opinion that Reese hadn't demonstrated his worth as her husband. He declared he wouldn't issue a dowry until he saw the depth of Reese's love for Evelyn with his own eyes. Evelyn didn't believe that would ever happen. After all, they had yet to share a marriage bed since the night they wed. She wondered if Reese knew of Uncle Theo's intentions.

"Will you join us tomorrow?"

Evelyn's gaze trailed across the room, not meeting Reese's eyes. She longed to spend time with him. Tomorrow's outing seemed to be the perfect opportunity to show him how she fit in with his family…

Who did she fool? Certainly not herself. She wouldn't deny herself a chance to be near him. Did this make her desperate? She no longer cared. Where Reese Worthington stood, she held no pride. She'd lost it when she gave herself to him. She had fallen under Reese's spell that long-ago winter's night when he pressed his lips against hers in a tease.

"Yes."

Reese's smile grew when Evelyn kept avoiding his gaze. Seducing her would be easier than he thought. He bet he could have her in his bed by tomorrow night if the picnic went as planned. He would reverse his gruff behavior and turn the charm on. If only Reese used the same charm at the house party that he used on that cold winter night. His goal at the house party had been one of a calculated measure. To gain the ownership of a foal. Since he lost, he would have to focus his goal on making Evelyn happy and making her think she held his love.

Then he could convince the Duke of Colebourne to release the funds from Evelyn's dowry. Reese wondered if she knew of her uncle's refusal. The Duke of Colebourne had sent Reese details of the settlement that would help ease Reese's financial burden. His only stipulation was Evelyn's happiness. The duke didn't believe Reese loved Evelyn. Reese wondered what Evelyn had disclosed of their current relationship to the duke. Had she informed her uncle of his cruel words? If she had, then Colebourne would never have written a settlement.

Reese had made an inquiry to Gray of his father's intentions, but his friend remained furious with him for seducing his cousin and for Reese's cruel words regarding Evelyn. It would seem he had no allies within the Colebourne family. He thought to plead his case to Sinclair, but Reese walked a fine line with him, too. Throughout the house party, when Reese thought that he was seducing Charlotte, Sinclair had been the victor. Since Sinclair had married the chit, his loyalty lay with his wife, and he wouldn't aide Reese.

"Excellent." Reese stepped forward, reaching for Evelyn's hand that was tightly wrapped around a book. He lifted it to his lips, pressing a soft kiss across her knuckles. "It shall be a day of pleasure that I am quite looking forward to."

Evelyn's hand trembled under Reese's lips. She tried pulling her hand free, but he held on. His thumb stroked back and forth across her palm. Evelyn felt her cheeks grow warm. When she lifted her gaze, Reese was regarding her with a look of desire. Her mouth opened on a sigh before she bit the sound back. However, he noticed and his gaze flared with passion. Then he pulled away, stepping back from Evelyn.

Reese turned away from the tempting Evelyn. He needed to leave her wondering if he had changed. To set her up to fall at his feet. He strode to the door connecting their room. Before he stepped through, her soft voice whispered to him.

"Goodnight, Reese."

He looked over his shoulder, winking at Evelyn. "Sweet dreams, my lovely Evelyn."

Evelyn released the sigh she had been holding and laid back against the cushions. She wrapped her hand around the one he had held and kissed. The warmth of Reese's fingers stroking across her skin still tingled, the current sizzling to her fingertips.

Reese must have felt the same charge. Didn't he?

Chapter Seven

Evelyn walked down the staircase at the designated hour to leave for the afternoon picnic, expecting the excited chatter of her new family. However, only silence welcomed her. The only person waiting was Reese.

Evelyn paused two steps up from the floor. She watched Reese pace back and forth, unaware of her presence. He appeared to be conversing with himself, his hands making his points valid with each swish through the air.

Reese paused and glanced up. When he saw her, the scowl on his face disappeared and was replaced by a charming smile. A smile charming enough that it distracted her from questioning his behavior.

Reese approached Evelyn, stopping on the step below hers, eager for their afternoon excursion. What a perfect opportunity to woo Evelyn with his family for company. Not only did he have to convince her that his attitude toward her was changing, but he must also redeem himself with his family. His treatment of Evelyn upset them. To pacify them, he needed to show how much he cared for Evelyn. Then they could help him convince her that he cared about her. If she could use her family to fool him, then why couldn't he use his family likewise?

"Am I late?" Evelyn asked.

He shook his head. "No. My family left early to find the perfect setting for your first visit to our favorite picnic spot. Maggie promised to wait to feed the ducklings until you arrived. But she also said to hurry. Shall we?"

"Yes, of course."

Evelyn fumbled with her bonnet. She tried to open the bonnet wider to set upon her head, but Reese's nearness flustered her. Her hands fumbled with the ribbons.

Reese pulled it from her hands and slipped it over her curls. After he tied the ribbon, he caressed her cheek, tucking a stray curl inside. He bent his head to place a kiss where he had touched her and whispered near her ear, "You look lovely today."

Evelyn held her breath, afraid she might have imagined his attention. When he pulled away with desire burning in his gaze, his warmth spread inside her, and she knew his attention was no illusion. She should stay on guard with his sudden change of attitude, but her knees weakened from his closeness. Her heart opened wider, craving his attention, needing it to survive. If she was a fool, then so be it.

"Thank you," she whispered.

A calm settled over Reese. He had been debating on how to proceed with Evelyn. Reese wondered how she would receive his attention. He doubted her open acceptance, fearing he had pushed her too hard with his coldness since they married. However, it was as if she held her arms open wide for him to land in. Was Evelyn so desperate for attention that she would accept any kindness he offered? If so, his plan would be easier than he thought. He only had to release his full arsenal of charm, and Evelyn would be his devoted slave.

Reese grabbed a hold of Evelyn's hand and guided her out to the curricle waiting for them. He helped her up into the high seat, making her comfortable for the bumpy ride they were about to embark on. After he settled himself, he took the ribbons and started their ride to the pond.

Along the way, he gave Evelyn a brief history of the estate and pointed out landmarks. She exclaimed her delight at the beauty of his home and asked him questions pertaining to the estate he hadn't considered himself. She surprised him with her knowledge of estate management. He was so enamored by their conversation, he didn't notice how near to the pond they were.

Reese's family waved to them, their excitement more than obvious. Suddenly, he felt nothing but disappointment. Now he had to share Evelyn with his family. He wished it were only the two of them. He wanted to share the magic of the area with her alone. The pond had always been an oasis of happiness for his family. It was the only place their father never visited. They would escape there throughout the year when they needed peace.

For the first time in his life, Reese experienced selfishness, and he wished his family weren't there. However, they had as much a right to share this little piece of paradise with Evelyn as he did, if not more so. He didn't deserve to at all, truth be told. His boorish behavior ruined his right. But still, that didn't keep him from wanting to share an afternoon wrapped in her sunshine.

Reese watched Evelyn's face brighten when she saw his family. Her adoration of them was obvious, as were theirs. His brother and sisters bombarded Evelyn with questions on her opinion of the estate. Evelyn laughed at their enthusiasm. Reese felt a twinge at her laughter and realized he was jealous of her openness with his family. Did he want her to be that carefree with him?

His twinge only grew tighter when Graham reached out and swung Evelyn from the curricle. Reese's grip tightened on the ribbons as he stared at Graham's hands wrapped around his wife's waist. Then when Evelyn's laughter grew and she rested her hands on Graham's shoulders, his twinge clenched again.

Graham swung Evelyn in a circle before releasing her, but he stayed close enough to her in case she lost her footing. Soon Noel and Eden hooked their arms through Evelyn's and dragged her to the pond where his mother and Maggie were feeding the ducklings.

Reese swung his head toward Graham's chuckle. He narrowed his eyes and growled at his brother, who in return let out a bellow of laughter.

"Mmm, that is what I thought. I was not for certain. But now I am."

"What do you imagine you are so certain of?" Reese growled.

His brother gave him a sly smile. "Why, your regard of the lovely Evelyn. She looks most exquisite today, does she not? Like sunshine bursting through the clouds. Yes, that is how I would describe her," Graham answered and walked away before Reese could dispute him.

Sunshine? Was that not how Reese just referred to Evelyn? Only Graham's description was more accurate than his. She had been a ray of sunshine to his family. Reese observed how his sisters clamored for her attention, each of them finding something in Evelyn that brightened their outlook on life. While he only thought to use her for a means to an end, they embraced her quiet manner for something altogether different.

Reese walked toward the pond and leaned against a tree, reflecting on his wife.

His mother interrupted his thoughts. "I hope your appearance at our picnic today is because you are welcoming Evelyn as your wife, not as a ploy for revenge against the charming girl."

Reese wanted to scoff at the "charming girl" comment. Devious would have been the more appropriate term. However, to convince Evelyn of his devotion, he must also convince his family, especially his mother. His mother was shrewd and would notice his intent if he didn't stay on guard.

"After a considerable amount of time, my anger with her deception has waned. I no longer hold any animosity toward Evelyn. I want to start anew. There could not have been a more splendid opportunity than to join my family in a picnic at our favorite spot." He glanced over at her. "Do you not agree it to be most fitting, Mother?"

His mother narrowed her gaze at him, looking for any sign of deception. When she noticed his innocent smile and how his gaze kept drifting toward Evelyn, she squeezed his arm in acceptance. "Yes, most fitting. I feared for a while you were following in your father's footsteps with your anger. I am glad that you have found reason and wish to make Evelyn your loving wife."

His mother strolled over to the girls and joined in with their laughter. Reese paused, contemplating his mother's words. She wasn't the first member of his family who had taunted him with that comparison. Graham and Eden had both thrown those words at him. And if Noel's frown toward him whenever they crossed was any indication, then she felt the same way. Only Maggie had treated him the same. Or had she? Now that he recalled, Maggie had been absent from joining him in the stables.

Reese looked toward his family and saw the reason they supported Evelyn. She had become one of them. Would he ever regard her in the same light? Or would he let his revenge ruin what could be an endearing relationship? Either way, he refused to consider it.

~~~~~~

"Your first picnic with Reese. Isn't it so romantic?" Noel gushed.

"Actually, we have already shared a picnic once before. Evelyn chose me to be her guest to share a picnic basket with during the house party."

Noel beamed. "Even more dreamy. Who else was at the picnic?"

Reese took a bite out of the chocolate cake everyone else devoured. He swallowed before speaking. "Everyone from the house party. However, Evelyn and I shared a blanket and basket of the most edible delights by ourselves. Did you know my wife has a sweet tooth for chocolate pudding?"

"Then we must have cook prepare the dessert for dinner," said his mother.

"I agree." Reese winked at Evelyn.

Noel continued romanticizing the picnic. "Did Reese read love poems to you? Did you gaze into each other's eyes?"

Evelyn shook her head. "No, we did not speak throughout the picnic. Your brother made moon eyes at my sister, Charlotte, and glared at her picnic companion, Lord Sinclair."

Silence descended on them. Evelyn could pinch herself for being so spiteful. It wasn't her intention. She made herself a promise not to lie or glamorize their relationship. His family needed to understand, Noel especially, that she had tricked Reese into marrying her.

Reese stared at her. "Had I known it was your kisses that set my soul on fire, I would have directed all my devotion toward you."

The other ladies sighed at his declaration, Graham laughed, and Evelyn only wanted to roll her eyes. She saw his attempt to charm her for what it was. He applied his tactics a little too heavy for Evelyn to believe his sincerity. He may fool his family, but not her. She'd had enough practice with Charlotte over the years to realize that her husband wanted his family to believe he had miraculously forgiven her. But Evelyn knew better.

What Reese didn't understand was that she loved him with every breath of her soul. She knew her husband's flaws and his little idiosyncrasies. When he pretended to play someone false, his tone held a flatness to it, as if he didn't believe in his lie. However, his voice deepened with passion when he spoke the truth. When he lied, he held his left hand in a fist. But if he told the truth, he used the same hand to speak with. Then there were his eyes. Reese's blue gaze held a dull flatness with his lies. However, if he believed in what he spoke, the sapphires shone with his sincerity.

Evelyn smiled sweetly at Reese, willing to play his game until she learned the rules. "I am sure you would have, Lord Worthington." She looked at Eden. "Would you care to join me for a walk? I wish to continue our discussion from yesterday."

Eden jumped up. "I would love to."

Reese watched Evelyn walk away with his sister. Eden pointed to landmarks near them, and Evelyn would laugh along with Eden's stories. Soon Maggie rose from the blanket and skipped after them. He sighed. He didn't know how to judge their conversation during lunch. Had Evelyn fallen for his false compliment?

"You try too hard, brother," said Graham.

"I agree," replied his mother.

"Perhaps, if you were more sincere, Evelyn might believe you. You are sincere, are you not, Reese?" asked Noel.

He didn't meet their gazes. "Why would I not be?"

"Your left hand is closed in a fist," said Graham, giving him a look.

Noel shrugged. "Your voice is flat. There was no passion when you spoke."

"And your eyes hold a dull expression. If your own family knows these characteristics when you lie, do you not think that the woman who loves you would notice these too?" asked his mother. "Which only confirms what I hoped was not true."

He sighed in frustration. "All of you misunderstand."

His mother smoothed her hands down her skirt. "Do we?"

"Yes, I feel awkward sharing my feelings toward Evelyn in front of my family. 'Tis all." He shrugged as if it were no big deal.

"Humph," answered Graham.

Noel reached out and wrapped her hands around Reese's fist, trying to coax his hand to relax. "It is your loss, Reese, if you choose not to forgive Evelyn. She has a heart full of love to give, if only you would give her the chance. If you will not, then one day she will find someone else who will."

Noel rose, since Reese wouldn't loosen his fist. Her smile held sadness for him before she wandered over to her sisters.

Noel's declaration left Reese speechless. When had his sister become so wise and capable of speaking with such clarity? He'd always thought of Noel as lighthearted and full of romantic fantasies. However, Noel held an insight that most of her age wouldn't.

"Your sister speaks the truth. I only hope you realize the gift given to you before it is too late."

His mother rose after her comment, and Graham followed. Graham offered their mother his arm and left Reese alone after they strolled away. Once again, Reese was an outsider to his own family, and Evelyn was more accepted than he was. When had his plan taken a turn for the worse? Was his mother correct and Evelyn knew that he played her false?

No, impossible. The girl hardly knew him at all.

Chapter Eight

Reese cleared the picnic area away. His family valued their privacy during their more intimate moments, so they never allowed the servants to accompany them to the pond. He hoped to atone for his behavior and maybe convince his family and Evelyn that he had changed. Perhaps he could convince Evelyn to join him for a boat ride. There, he would have her alone and could gauge her reaction to see if she had fallen for his charm.

Soon his family arrived back from their walk. He waited for any sign of forgiveness with his hands behind his back. They stopped talking once they came upon him, making it more than obvious that he had been the topic of their discussion. Reese reined in his annoyance at being their subject of ridicule.

"Evelyn, can I interest you in a row around the pond? Around the bend of trees, there is a view of the estate I think you will enjoy," asked Reese.

"What a splendid idea," said Noel, winking at Reese from behind Evelyn.

Reese bit back a smile at his sister's attempt to convince Evelyn to spend time alone with him.

They left Evelyn with no choice but to accept Reese's offer. If she showed displeasure at his attempt to repair their marriage, then his family would lay the fault on her. If she accepted, it didn't mean Evelyn forgave him or believed Reese wanted to fix their marriage.

Reese held his breath, awaiting her refusal.

"I would love to," Evelyn answered, and he felt only the tiniest twinge of guilt.

Evelyn followed Reese to the paddle boat, and with Graham's help, she sat across from Reese while he tested the paddles in the water. Assured they were workable, he paddled them from the clearing. After waving to the family, Evelyn focused her attention on her husband, curious as to why he suggested they spend time alone. However, he never spoke, leaving her disappointed. He worked the rows with his body relaxed and a serene smile settled upon his face. Evelyn had never seen Reese in such a lighthearted mood. It was as if the weight of the world had been lifted from his shoulders, and he was enjoying the simplicity of the day.

She decided to relax her guard and accept his offer for what it was. A time to relax and take pleasure in each other with the beauty of the estate surrounding them. It was a magnificent sight. The trees were full. The wildflowers were blooming and dotted the countryside with its abundance of color. Ducklings swam alongside the boat, causing Evelyn to giggle at their antics.

When Reese looked her way, Evelyn pointed to the ducks. His face lit up with one of his swooning smiles. Only his smile didn't just come from his kissable lips, but his eyes shone with humor, drawing Evelyn under his spell. Her fate was doomed.

Reese rowed them to the opening beyond the trees. The sight in front of him never seemed to amaze him. His property stretched out for miles in splendid beauty. When he was younger, he'd visited this spot often, dreaming of when it would all be his. Now that the day had come, and the view held even more glory. He glanced at Evelyn to see if her reaction was the same.

Evelyn looked in awe at the gorgeous landscape. She'd grown up on an amazing estate, but it didn't hold the raw beauty of Reese's home. The rolling hills in the landscape begged for you to roam them, and the wildflowers whispered for you to pick them. Evelyn imagined exploring the wildness with Reese and their children.

"There are no words to describe the beauty of your home, Reese." Evelyn spoke with such sincerity that it choked her up.

Reese reached across the boat and slid his hands in hers. "Our home, Evelyn. This beauty now belongs to you, too."

Reese watched the blush spread over her cheeks. When she tried to pull her hands away, he held on tight. He meant every word he said, and he wanted her to at least believe him on this. His home was now hers and would be the home of their children. A home that he hoped in time would be free of deception and revenge. That might have been hypocritical of his current plans, yet it was how he felt at this moment.

Evelyn didn't answer Reese. She kept staring at their joined hands, then flitting away to the scenery, then back to their hands. The warmth and comfort from his touch swept away Evelyn's doubts on Reese's agenda. He couldn't embrace the beauty of this land that he now shared with her and not have forgiven her.

Soon their peaceful afternoon took a turn for the worse. The dark clouds closed in, and a burst of rain showered down upon them. Reese cursed, causing Evelyn to laugh at him. He shook his head and growled at the sky, but soon started laughing along with her. Her enjoyment at their predicament consumed Reese. He wanted to capture more of the free spirit he didn't know Evelyn held.

"Is the rain part of what makes this view so special?" Evelyn teased.

Reese couldn't answer her. The rain only enhanced the beauty of Evelyn. Rain dripped along her cheeks and drifted to her lips, leaving little droplets of water waiting for him to lick away. Her emerald eyes shone with flecks of fairy dust. Silver sparkles pulled him closer. Her laughter burst with a melody against the thunder crackling. Reese leaned forward, brushing a wet strand from her cheeks.

"So very special," Reese murmured before tracing his tongue across her lips, tasting the sweet drops of rain upon them.

When Evelyn sighed, Reese wrapped his hand around the back of her neck, pulling her into his kiss. Her lips opened under his, and Reese devoured her. One kiss after another. He savored the intoxicating flavor of Evelyn. Raindrops, chocolate cake, and passion. With every one of Evelyn's kisses, she poured her soul into him, and Reese greedily accepted them, never wanting it to end.

Evelyn trembled, and Reese thought it was from the passion they shared. But when her teeth started clattering against his, he realized it was from the chill in the air. He pulled away and noticed her body shook from her drenched clothing. Reese swore again at his callous disregard for her care.

He pulled off his coat and wrapped it around her. "I'll get us inside soon. Just a little longer."

Reese rowed them toward the small cottage nestled between the trees that the family used when they came ice skating in the winter. He searched for his family in the downpour to see if they took up shelter, but all he noticed was Graham's horse tied near the cottage. The other conveyances were gone. His family had abandoned them. When Evelyn started sneezing, Reese rowed harder, only for the oars to split in half. Was their afternoon destined for one disaster after another?

Evelyn shivered under Reese's coat, watching him row them closer to shelter. His determination to see to her welfare comforted her and convinced her that Reese cared. When he stood and the boat shook, Evelyn grabbed onto the sides. "Reese?"

"The oars broke."

"How?"

"Graham," Reese growled.

She frowned. "Why?"

Reese shook his head, refusing to answer his wife on why his brother would damage their only means to safety. The interfering sneak. Then he realized his family was behind the sabotage, and it explained their absence. When he carried Evelyn into the cottage, he knew everything for a proper seduction would be present. He looked ahead and noted the smoke rising from the chimney. Yes, they had set a fire, and Reese was positive that there would be blankets and pillows laid near the hearth. Also, they would leave provisions to get them through the night.

 He didn't know whether to keep cursing his bad luck or thank his family for the help in seducing his wife.

"Reese?" Evelyn said again, staring at him.

Reese realized he needed to reward his family for his gratitude. They made his plan progress sooner than he'd hoped for. At this instant, his plan no longer mattered. He wanted Evelyn with an ache he didn't understand but knew he needed to fulfill.

"Only a trick to seek his revenge. Nothing to concern yourself over."

"How will we get to the bank?"

"Like this."

Reese jumped in the water, which only hit him at the waist. Then he started pulling the boat toward land. Once he secured the boat, he lifted Evelyn and carried her to the cottage. Even though her clothing left her soaked, her warmth seared into him. She wrapped her arms around his neck and settled her head on his shoulder. Evelyn's trust humbled him. He didn't deserve one ounce of it. But like the greedy bastard he was, Reese would take it and use it to his advantage and worry over the consequences of it later.

When he arrived at the cottage, he noticed the door ajar. Reese kicked the door open and stepped inside. As he thought, a fire warmed the hearth, and a variety of blankets and pillows were spread across the floor. A bottle of wine rested on the table with two glasses and a picnic basket he'd not seen before. Ahh, his family was so predictable.

How would Evelyn react to the seduction scene?

Reese slid her down his body, and Evelyn kept her hands wrapped behind his neck. He didn't want to give her a chance to see what awaited them. He wanted to sweep her into the passion they always shared once their lips met.

He took her mouth in a gentle kiss, coaxing Evelyn to open herself to their desire. His hands worked on sliding off her bonnet and unbuttoning her dress. When he freed the buttons, he lowered the dress off her shoulders. When the warm air brushed against her shivering body, Evelyn pulled away and raised her eyes to his. Her questioning gaze pierced him, leaving Reese hanging onto a fear that she would refuse his advances.

Evelyn wasn't questioning Reese. His intentions were more than clear. And his family's, too. They had set her up for Reese's seduction. Was this set up for Reese, too? Or had it been at his request? No. She didn't believe so. Evelyn stood there, questioning herself. Should she give herself to a man she didn't trust to return her love? Or should she refuse whatever Reese wanted to give her?

Evelyn ached for any sign from Reese that he had forgiven her, and today had proved a step in that direction. His gaze reflected his fear of her refusal. Did he realize the full impact of his emotions regarding her? She knew in her heart that he hadn't accepted her apology, but he would. But did Reese understand that? Evelyn doubted it. If so, he wouldn't look conflicted by his actions.

Evelyn slid out of her wet dress, letting it hit the floor in a puddle. She took two steps back and slid her chemise off. Reese stood rooted, unsure of Evelyn. She smiled, taking two more steps closer to the fire. Evelyn bent over and slid a stocking off before backing up again.

This time, Reese advanced a few steps then stopped. Evelyn took off her other stocking, leaving a trail behind her. Turning around, she strolled to stand naked before the fire. She heard Reese approach. He came to stand but a whisper away from her. When Reese lifted a hand to trail from her shoulder to her breasts, his hand trembled.

~~~~~~

One hour earlier

"Mama, the rain clouds are coming." Maggie pointed to the sky.

"Yes, I see that dear. We must get started on our return home."

"What about Reese and Evelyn? Should we warn them?" Maggie asked.

Lady Worthington watched her son row farther away, oblivious to the impending storm. His attention was devoted to his wife. The storm wasn't the only factor Reese was oblivious to. He was clueless to the emotions his wife stirred in him. With a little push, he would soon realize the impact Evelyn had over him. And today was one of those days to gently nudge him in Evelyn's direction.

A devious smile lit her face. "They will be fine, dear. Graham, is everything prepared?"

"Yes. I've set the scene," Graham answered.

"Can we not wait in the cottage for the rain to pass?" Noel asked.

Eden smirked. "No, we cannot. Mama and Graham have prepared the cottage for Reese and Evelyn."

Noel frowned. "How so?"

"One of a romantic nature," her mother told her mysteriously. "Now, we need to leave before the storm comes down upon us. Graham, leave your horse for Reese and Evelyn. Maggie, you ride with Graham in Reese's curricle. Noel and Eden, we will take the cart back."

"Mother, Evelyn is afraid of horses," Eden reprimanded.

Lady Worthington smiled patiently. "Yes, I am aware of her fear. This is an opportunity for your brother to show his wife that he will protect her from her fears. To allow him to show that he is not the insensitive brute he has shown himself to be. Let it be known, girls, that any gentleman who isn't sensitive to your fears isn't worthy of your love."

"I must remember to never bring my bride around once I get married," said Graham.

"Probably for the best if you decide to follow your brother's lead," agreed Lady Worthington.

"If I am ever so lucky to win a lady's love from someone as exquisite as Evelyn, I will worship at her feet."

Lady Worthington nodded in approval. She knew her younger son would devote his life to the woman he loved. He had always been a charmer with a heart full of love. No matter what rumors floated their way from London about his womanizing ways. Once Graham found his soul mate, there would be no doubt of his devotion.

Reese, on the other hand, had always held himself above love. Oh, he cared deeply about his family, but he was the only child who had faced his father's vindictiveness. He had dealt with the brunt of his father's rages, infidelity toward her, and their financial ruin all by himself. Reese had hardened his heart a little more than most. She hoped in time that he would understand how Evelyn gave her love to him freely with no strings attached.

Until then, she would help steer Reese along the right path and not the one his father had traveled.

Thunder crackled overhead, and they hurried along. Lady Worthington looked over her shoulder at the smoke rising from the cottage and smiled in satisfaction. Now it was up to Reese to initiate the seduction scene. Or Evelyn, for that matter.

~~~~~

Reese stood behind Evelyn and drew in her essence. The warmth of the fire breathed life to her fragrance, wrapping Reese in its gentle embrace. He had frozen when she backed away from him. He feared he had taken his advances too far, that it was too soon. Instead, she'd undressed like a siren, her seductive steps moving backwards, enticing him to follow.

When she turned her back to him, Reese awoke from his trance and strode to her side.

Evelyn turned to him. Surprise reflected in her gaze at his closeness. Her silken skin beckoned him to caress her softness. Starting at her shoulders, he stroked a path to her plump breasts, and she trembled under his touch. Or it could have been he who trembled for the chance to savor Evelyn. He brushed his thumb across her tight bud, back and forth. Evelyn sighed. When he pressed his thumb and finger and twisted, Evelyn gasped and his mouth crashed into hers, swallowing her moans.

His other hand reached up to capture her other breast. He stroked them until Evelyn writhed before him. Her kisses begged him to love her with each stroke of her tongue against his. Still, Evelyn never once touched Reese. He burned, ached with a need only Evelyn could fulfill with her gentle caresses. Reese needed her touch upon him, her fingers trailing across his body, her kisses whispering against his skin.

Reese lifted Evelyn in his arms and carried her to the pillows. He laid her down gently and sat back on his heels, taking in her beauty. Her hair lay in rivulets across her shoulders, soaked from the rain. Evelyn's body glowed in the fire's light. She was exquisite, and she was his.

"Do you want me to stop?"

Reese's gruff voice echoed his doubt. Evelyn hoped it wasn't from her not touching him. She lost the ability to function once Reese touched her, her senses exploding with every sensuous caress and kiss. Even now, with his intense stare, Evelyn couldn't complete a thought, let alone move. But then she noticed her silence and neglect.

Evelyn needed to show Reese how much she needed him to continue.

Evelyn rose to her knees, shaking her head at his question. When he still didn't look satisfied, she started unbuttoning his shirt. When she reached the last button, she lifted his shirt off. Then she trailed her fingers from his shoulder, across his chest, and down to the inside of his trousers, where she ran back and forth. Her hand dipped lower, and Reese sucked in a breath when she brushed across his hardness. His need for her was more than evident.

Evelyn's siren smile returned when she touched Reese's cock. All his doubts fled with that one curious caress. He imagined how he would react if she were to take hold and pleasure him the way he craved. But he couldn't ask that of Evelyn. She was his wife, not his whore. Still, it didn't keep him from wondering how the soft touch of her lips guiding him deeper into her mouth would feel. Heaven. Pure heaven with a touch of madness.

Evelyn wanted to touch Reese as intimately as he touched her, but her shyness kept her from exploring more. Instead, she moved to safer territories and let her hands wander up the length of his back until they sank in his damp strands. Evelyn coaxed Reese to lower his head, so she could answer him with her kiss. Her tongue trailed across his lips, dipping inside then back out again. Teasing him with a taste, then pulling away.

However, her husband lost patience with her sweet torture and took control of the kiss. He dominated their passion with each stroke of his tongue. Evelyn whimpered under his kiss, losing herself once again to Reese.

Evelyn's teasing undid him. His passion had been unleashed, and he needed to make Evelyn his again. Now. He swept her under him, spreading her legs apart. His hands lowered, sweeping up her thighs to find her wet for him. Reese sunk a finger inside, and Evelyn's fire singed him. He tore open the placket of his trousers, pulled out his cock, and guided it toward the heat. He wanted to take her quick, but stopped when he realized he wanted to savor each sensation of sliding inside her while Evelyn's heat surrounded him. She rewarded Reese with her body's response of pleasure.

Evelyn thrust her body at Reese, her pussy tightening around his cock, gripping him with its softness. She arched her hips into his, her body begging him to stroke her harder. She clutched at his arms while her legs locked around his, sliding up and down with the anticipation of fulfillment.

"Reese," Evelyn whispered.

With each touch from Reese, Evelyn's desire grew higher, yet still out of reach. Reese took possession of her body with each stroke. She rode toward the edge of completeness that she only wanted to reach with Reese. His strokes turned bolder, demanding Evelyn's surrender. He built in her a need so powerful, it frightened her until he reached a peak and soothed her with a gentleness her body craved.

Evelyn moaned. "Reese."

His passion kept climbing. Each stroke wasn't enough for him. Evelyn had only whispered and moaned his name. His need to have her scream his name in ecstasy drove him to take full possession of her soul. He needed to hear her screams as he needed air to breathe. To him, they were the signs of her surrendering to the passion that pushed them into completeness.

Reese paused, watching his wife on the brink of surrendering, her head thrown back, little whimpers escaping between her lips as her body clung to him. He swiveled his hips, pressing himself in deeper. Her eyes widened at the pressure, capturing his gaze. With each press closer, Evelyn arched into him. She tightened her core around his cock, and each throb vibrated with her need. When her nails dug into his back, Reese lost what control he held onto. He drove into Evelyn, unleashing his possession.

"Reese!" Evelyn screamed.

Evelyn screamed Reese's name over and over when his body took control and satisfied the craving her body needed that only Reese could fulfill. She gave her body freely—and her heart, whether or not he wanted it. It was his, and no other would hold it in their hands. Evelyn had lost herself to Reese.

Evelyn's scream sank into Reese's soul and took hold, never to let go. They were fated to be one, as much as Reese kept trying to deny it. Each time he made love to Evelyn, their bond strengthened. What confused him was that he didn't want to release the hold. He craved to see how much tighter it would wound itself.

He gathered Evelyn close, not ready to let her go, before he drifted to sleep.

Evelyn, wrapped in Reese's embrace, lay in awe of their powerful connection. She heard Reese's light snores and snuggled closer. She knew this afternoon was a rare occurrence for their marriage and decided she would indulge in the pleasure for as long as possible instead of denying herself. Until the day she needed to make a decision regarding the fate of their marriage. But for now, she would seek the comfort she craved from his arms.

Chapter Nine

Evelyn hummed as she arranged the flowers in the foyer. It was a small task she had taken upon herself once she realized how much Reese loved the smell of fresh-cut flowers. It was an extra touch to her most recent changes that he approved of. Reese was never stingy with his compliments regarding how she had taken over her wifely duties, especially in the bedroom.

Every night since the picnic, Reese had come to her bedroom and carried her to his, where he made passionate love to her before carrying Evelyn back to her own bed to sleep. While Evelyn yearned to spend the night in his arms, she didn't protest. A cocoon of forgiveness surrounded them. She didn't want to disrupt it, for fear that their marriage would become strained again.

An arm wrapped around her middle, and Evelyn sighed, leaning back against Reese. His warm lips kissed a path along her neck.

"While the flowers are a lovely touch to the foyer, they pale compared to the beauty of my wife," he whispered in her ear.

She melted in his arms. Reese turned Evelyn around and kissed her softly. However, one simple kiss wasn't enough. He desired to carry her abovestairs, lay her on his bed, and worship her all afternoon. He raised his head, looking for any sign of his family. If they weren't around, he could make his wish come true.

"Graham took your mother and sisters into the village to shop."

"Did you not wish to join them? I have informed the shopkeepers to add your name to my accounts."

"There is nothing I desire in the village stores, my lord. All that I desire is right here." Evelyn looked down shyly, running her fingers along the buttons of his waistcoat.

"And the servants?" Reese gulped when Evelyn's fingers trailed lowered.

Evelyn stood on her tiptoes, her lips trailing up his neck. This time she whispered in his ears, "I suppose they are taking their luncheon."

Evelyn stepped back, giving Reese a lingering glance before she started walking up the stairs. Reese stood spellbound by his aggressive wife and watched her pause halfway up. How he ever thought his wife dull was beyond him. Evelyn kept surprising him at every turn, leaving him in doubt of his revenge.

"Reese," Evelyn whispered.

"Mmm."

Evelyn laughed. "I have already whispered your name, which only leaves my moans and screams for you to listen to. Unless your afternoon is full?"

Evelyn started back down the steps, but soon Reese threw her over his shoulder, taking the stairs two at a time. Evelyn's laughter filled the house when she heard Reese muttering about having a tease for a wife. Before they reached the landing, someone pounded on the door, letting them know a visitor had arrived. Reese paused only long enough until the pounding stopped, then he continued to his bedroom. However, before he reached the entry, the pounding began again, and no servants rushed to answer the door.

"Reese, the servants are at lunch. We must answer. Something could have happened to your family and they need our help."

"Nonsense, Graham is with them. It is probably a busybody neighbor wanting to meet my wife. I will not share you this afternoon."

Evelyn's heart warmed at Reese's declaration. She almost forgot about answering the door and considered allowing Reese to draw her into his bedroom. After all, it was at her suggestion that he follow her. However, whoever pounded on the door was relentless.

"Reese," Evelyn persisted.

Reese sighed his frustration. A more inviting afternoon without his family around would seldom happen again. His opportunity was wasted by a simple knock on the door. Whoever they were, they had better have one hell of an explanation for ruining his pleasure.

Reese stomped down the stairs with Evelyn following him, her laughter floating behind. Reese wanted to enjoy Evelyn's playful mood in the bedroom. He threw open the door and growled at his guests. His worst nightmare stood on the stoop wearing a mischievous grin, and her cohort standing next to her wore a smirk at Reese's displeasure. He growled his welcome.

His wife peeked around him and exclaimed her glee. "Charlie!"

One hand pushed him away while another hand pulled him back, each lady trying to reach the other while he stood in their way. Evelyn wrapped her arms around Charlotte and twirled her around. Their chatter exploded around them, each asking questions and answering without drawing a breath. If Reese thought his wife a beauty that none could compare to before, she stood breathtaking now. The love Evelyn held for her sister was clear in every aspect of her affection. A love he envied and wished she held for him. Reese shook himself at such nonsense.

Sinclair cleared his throat behind him. When he looked over his shoulder, he narrowed his eyes at Sinclair's know-it-all expression. Sinclair stood waiting for an invitation into his home, one Reese had no inclination of extending, even though Sinclair's wife had made herself welcome. At Reese's glare, Sinclair only laughed.

"Ah, I know the feeling," said Sinclair.

Reese rolled his eyes. "I highly doubt it."

Sinclair shrugged. "You will get used to it."

"I have no intention now or in the future."

"You are still not sour on marrying Evelyn, are you?" asked Charlotte.

"Of course, he is not. Are you, my dear?" Evelyn asked, laying her hand on Reese's arm.

Reese didn't answer Evelyn's or Charlotte's questions. Was he still angry with her? Evelyn wondered when Reese tensed under her hand and continued scowling at their guests. The happy existence she had convinced herself of evaporated into the animosity from before. The last few weeks disappeared because her sister and brother-in-law had paid a visit. Evelyn stepped back from Reese, not trusting herself around the fury emanating from him.

Charlotte glared at Worthington's rude welcoming. Her uncle was correct about the earl. When she first arrived, her sister had displayed a playful complexion. Now Evelyn stepped away from Worthington, holding the same expression of sadness as when she'd confessed her deception.

Then there was the matter of Worthington. Fury rippled off him worse than when he'd visited Uncle Theo's estate. Charlotte was so thankful when her husband had suggested they pay a visit to Evelyn on their way to London. She hoped to convince Evelyn to join them on their journey. Now she made herself a promise that she wouldn't leave without Evelyn. Her sister didn't deserve such harsh treatment.

Charlotte thought her sister had found the same love she experienced with Sinclair. Her letters over the last few weeks had mentioned Reese this and Reese that. Evelyn had filled her lighthearted missives with descriptions of her duties as Reese's wife and of his wonderful family. Evelyn had seemed happy.

However, Evelyn's letters hadn't convinced Uncle Theo, and he wanted to see for himself. Charlotte had convinced her uncle that when they delivered the colt, they would stay for a visit to discover if Evelyn held the same happiness she portrayed. Lucas had wanted to come with them, but the anger he held toward his friend remained strong. Sinclair had convinced Lucas that he would give them a full report once they reached London.

"To what do we owe this pleasure?" Worthington snarled.

"We have set our path for London and we wished to deliver your wedding present along the way," answered Sinclair.

"I will take my leave. I have no desire to accept anything for an incident I still find distaste with." With that, Worthington stalked away, leaving the three of them alone.

Evelyn stood in shock at his departure. Her heart, which had mended, was now torn asunder once again. Their loving relationship had been a farce. But what was the reason for his deception? Had it all been for revenge? Apparently so.

Charlotte turned to Sinclair. "Worthington affirmed my decision to gift the paperwork to Evelyn alone. He wasn't worthy of the gift, Jasper. I know you meant well and wanted a peace offering, but as you have seen for yourself, it was for naught. Worthington has held onto his cruelty."

Sinclair ran a hand through her hair. "You are correct as usual, my dear. However, we should not focus on Worthington at this time. Evelyn needs our attention. She appears most distraught."

"Evelyn?" Charlotte asked.

"Mmm," said Evelyn, her head turned from watching Reese disappear to Charlotte and Sinclair.

"Are you well?"

Evelyn tried to smile. "Yes. Shall we have tea?"

She walked away without waiting for a reply. Charlotte and Sinclair followed her into a parlor and sat on the settee as Evelyn asked a servant to bring tea and a tray of refreshments. She settled on a chair near them and smiled serenely, her joy at their visit apparent. Still, her eyes held a sadness that only one person could make disappear. However, it was a wish that would never come true.

"So tell me, how are you enjoying married life? Are Jacqueline, Gemma, and Abigail prepared for the season? When are they arriving in London? Did Uncle Theo set a date for Lucas and Selina's wedding yet?" Evelyn bombarded them with questions to distract them from asking after her wellbeing. Her emotions were too delicate to explore, and she didn't want their sympathy. Not after she had written home about her happiness with Reese. A happiness that now proved false.

Charlotte knew Evelyn didn't wish to discuss Worthington's treatment in front of Jasper. After they visited for a brief spell, Charlotte would send Jasper away so she could have a private moment with her sister. For now, Charlotte answered Evelyn's questions, trying to make her laugh at their family's antics.

"Why did Lucas refuse to set a wedding date?" asked Evelyn.

Charlotte rolled her eyes. "He spouted off some nonsense about letting the girls enjoy their season, and he didn't want to steal away from their debut. I think he is trying to find a way out of the betrothal. You should see how jealous he has behaved since the house party."

"Abigail?"

"Yes. Jasper has introduced her to some gentlemen in the neighboring counties. They have taken an interest in Abigail, and she finds their company amiable. Why, at our wedding party, Abigail had her hand claimed for every dance. Lucas was in such a fit that night." Charlotte laughed.

"Now, what is this nonsense about a wedding present? We agreed no gifts," said Evelyn.

"I know, but Jasper wanted to make a grand gesture. You tell her," said Charlotte, bouncing in her seat with excitement.

Sinclair smiled fondly at his wife. "Our gift to you, Evelyn, is Cobalt."

"Sapphire's offspring?" Evelyn squeaked. "What am I to do with a horse?"

Sinclair shifted in his seat. "It was my intent to make a peaceful gesture toward your husband for the confusion of your, um…mistaken courtship. To let bygones be bygones and start our family anew. But from his earlier display, Worthington has not changed, and I agree with my wife that the paperwork should remain in your name."

Evelyn sighed. She had no excuse to give them for Reese's behavior. In truth, her mind was exhausted from trying to understand his sudden change of mood. "Thank you for your thoughtful gift. This wonderful news will thrill my husband once he hears of your generosity. Will you continue to London now?"

Charlotte gave Evelyn a hopeful smile. "We were hoping you would invite us to stay for an extended visit. I have missed you so much and want to spend time with you before I must face London without you." Charlotte shuddered at the morbid thought.

Evelyn laughed for the first time since they arrived. Charlotte found proper behavior to be an inconvenience. Charlotte would turn London on its ear with her unconventional antics, a sight Evelyn would miss but couldn't wait to hear about.

Evelyn brightened a little. "Excellent, I shall have a bedroom prepared for your stay. Reese's family is in the village this afternoon, and you can meet them at dinner. I love them so. They have been most welcoming."

Charlotte smirked. "Well, if their behavior is the opposite of Worthington's, then I am sure we will love them too."

"Charlie," Sinclair warned. "On that note, I shall take my leave. I need to speak with the stable master about Cobalt's care and to help him into his new home. You ladies need some time alone." Sinclair rose.

"I will have a footman guide you to the stables."

Sinclair waved her off. "No need, Evelyn. I have visited Worthington's estate before and I am familiar with my way around."

Jasper bent over and kissed Charlotte before he left. After he walked away, Charlotte stared after her husband with a dreamy expression. Evelyn felt a stab of envy, then brushed it away. She only held happiness for the love her sister shared with Jasper. It wasn't Charlotte's fault that Evelyn had married a toad. Obviously, the many kisses they'd shared hadn't turned him into a prince, but an evil villain instead.

Evelyn rose, walked to the doorway, and instructed a footman to inform the housekeeper to prepare a bedroom for Charlotte and Jasper. When she returned to take a seat, Charlotte held out her hand to join her on the settee. Evelyn grabbed onto the offer and settled near her, laying her head on Charlotte's shoulder.

"Do you wish to cry?" asked Charlotte.

"No. I have cried enough over him. He is no longer worth my tears." Evelyn sniffled.

"If you wish to, I am here and I promise not to judge. Even though I suggest we plot his demise. Much more of a productive solution."

Evelyn laughed. Charlotte had always been the more devious of the two and always strived to correct a wrong. Many victims had fallen under her crafty revenge. However, Evelyn couldn't allow Charlotte to retaliate, even if it would be pleasurable to watch. No, Evelyn needed to stand up for herself if she ever hoped to earn Reese's respect one day. She would think of her own plan to bring her husband to heel. If her plan didn't work, then she would seek Charlotte's advice. For now, she only wanted a sympathetic ear for her heartache.

Charlotte took her hand. "Your recent letters stated that Worthington had forgiven your deception, and you felt that he might love you."

Evelyn sighed. "It is what my husband led me to believe. But now I realize it was a false sense of security. He fooled me as I had fooled him. I would say we are even, but I do not believe he feels the same."

"Insufferable brute."

Evelyn laughed, "I am so happy you came. I have missed you too."

"And I you, Evie."

Evelyn growled. She hated that nickname.

She pulled away. She wanted to see Charlotte's reaction when she described her intimacy with Reese. She wanted to know if her behavior in the bedroom was normal or if her husband might think her too fast.

"What I do not understand is that only moments before you arrived, we had been about to…well, you know." Evelyn twisted her hand in the air to emphasize what she couldn't bring herself to say.

"No, what were you about to do?" Charlotte asked with an innocent smile. However, the teasing twinkle in her gaze gave her away.

Evelyn hit her with a pillow when she saw Charlotte's amusement. "Make love in the middle of the afternoon," Evelyn whispered, a blush spreading across her cheeks.

Charlotte relaxed back against the cushions. "Love in the afternoon when passion takes control is heavenly."

"Then Sinclair and you … ahh …"

Charlotte cocked an eyebrow. "Make love in the afternoon?"

Evelyn ducked her head. "Mmm, yes."

"The morning, afternoon, and throughout the night. Whenever the mood strikes. Yes, a lot." Charlotte winked.

"So, it is normal to …" Evelyn struggled to complete sentences.

"For a happy marriage? Most definitely."

"Ever since the picnic where Reese showed me his estate, we have had this newfound connection. Not a night has not gone by without him carrying me away to his bed or a day without his tender affection." Evelyn looked down at her hands, her heart heavy. "Why the sudden change?"

Charlotte pursed her lips. "I am afraid our visit has reminded Worthington of our deceit. Perhaps we should not stay."

"Nonsense. If my husband refuses to forgive something that happened in the past now, then he never will. I refuse to spend the rest of my life never being able to have my family around because it hurts his tender emotions."

Evelyn rose and started pacing the parlor, her stride taking her back and forth in front of Charlotte. Each time, she paused, attempting to voice her thoughts. Then she would shake her head and continue her path across the rug. It was on her tenth time across the room that the parlor doors swung open and Reese's family invaded the room.

Evelyn changed her flustered appearance to one of a serene demeanor. However, her mother-in-law noticed her state and offered her a smile full of sympathy.

Graham strode in behind his family, looking at a piece of mail, and didn't see Charlotte sitting on the settee. "Did you find out who the carriage belongs to, Mother?"

"I believe Evelyn's sister is paying us a visit," answered Lady Worthington.

Graham's gaze raised to stare at the identical twins. "Holy …"

Charlotte rose and linked her arms with Evelyn, laughing at Graham's reaction.

"Graham!" Eden exclaimed.

Graham blinked. "Well … I … ah …"

Evelyn took pity on Graham and made the introductions. She explained how Charlotte and Sinclair were dropping off a wedding present on their way to London for the upcoming season. She added how she had invited her family to stay for a few days. Everyone agreed it was a wonderful idea to give them a chance to know one another better.

"Can I see your present, Evelyn?" Maggie asked.

Evelyn smiled. "I am afraid I cannot show you. You will have to visit the stables if you wish to see the present. It is a new colt named Cobalt."

Graham looked at her in surprise. "Is this the same foal my brother thought he had won?"

"The very same." Charlotte winked at Graham.

Graham whistled. "I guess that explains his absence."

Charlotte fisted her hands on her hips. "Yes. No offense to your family, but your brother's manners are despicable. He behaved most rudely at our arrival."

"Yes, that sounds like Reese," agreed Eden.

Evelyn grew quieter at their description of Reese, not wanting to draw attention her way. She didn't want Reese's family to notice her heartache. However, her new family was more attuned to Evelyn's moods than she realized.

"Evelyn?" Noel asked.

"Yes, dear?"

"Are you well?"

Evelyn's smiled wistfully. "Yes. I am emotional after visiting with my sister for the first time in months. I did not realize how much I have missed Charlotte."

Evelyn's answer seemed to pacify everyone. Or so she thought.

"Shall we take a walk to the stable to welcome the newest addition to our family, Mags?" asked Graham.

Maggie jumped from her chair with excitement and pulled Graham from his. She led him from the room, forgetting her manners on asking permission to leave. They could hear Maggie's excited chatter all the way down the hallway. Everyone in the room laughed. Maggie reminded Evelyn of Charlotte.

"Was I like that at her age?" asked Charlotte.

"You still are." Evelyn laughed.

~~~~~

Reese stood against the fence, watching Sinclair walk the colt around the open field. He didn't know whether to refuse or accept the gift. His pride kept from doing either. Did Sinclair offer him the gift out of pity? Or was it, as Sinclair stated, a peace offering? Either way, he would be a fool to refuse such an offer. This opened up the possibilities for his breeding program's success.

Still, it didn't erase the circumstances he found himself in. He had a wife who confused the hell out of him. One moment, he wanted to kneel at her feet and adore her. The next moment, he wrestled with his demons on destroying her for her deceit and making him look like a fool. However, his need for revenge kept slipping away more and more every day. For a while there, they had existed in this peaceful harmony. Then *poof*, it disappeared by one simple visit from her family. He'd behaved rudely earlier, but he refused to apologize.

He turned his attention back to what was happening. The colt was a beauty. He admired its fine lines and graceful gait. He wondered about its speed once fully grown. Would the horse fly across the fields or racetrack? Only time would tell.

Before long, Maggie and Graham joined him to watch Sinclair run the colt through a workout. Reese's trainer stood nearby, listening to Sinclair's instructions.

"He is so beautiful," Maggie said, awed.

Reese nodded in agreement. "Yes, he is."

"Can I help Lord Sinclair?" Maggie asked.

Reese whistled for Sinclair and pointed to Maggie, then to the horse. Sinclair nodded, waving for Maggie to join him. Maggie let out a holler and climbed over the fence, running toward Sinclair and the horse. Reese chuckled at his sister's excitement. He watched Sinclair patiently explain to Maggie about the colt's care. Sinclair lowered himself to Maggie's height and talked softly to her about what Cobalt enjoyed. Cobalt. A fitting name for the colt, especially after having a mother named Sapphire.

"That is one hell of a present," Graham commented.

Reese ignored his brother, hoping Graham would go away. However, he wasn't so lucky.

His brother slung his arm over the rung of the fence and settled himself in for the duration. "Please explain how you could not tell Evelyn and Charlotte apart? They are as different as night and day. Even down to their laughter."

Reese sighed. He knew he would find no peace until Graham had his say. Reese would have to listen to this torture because Graham would be persistent until he did. "How are they different?"

"Well, one difference is that Charlotte has this throaty seductive laughter that tempts you with an adventure. While Evelyn's laughter is soft and sensual, drawing you into her spell." He turned to face Reese. "Then there are their mannerisms. Charlotte has an unconventional approach to life. I think with Charlotte you must always be on edge, waiting for the unexpected. While Evelyn is a lady to most admire. Her grace speaks volumes. Not that there is anything wrong with Charlotte. However, she does not appear to be your type. At least from the choice of your mistresses in the past."

Reese blew a breath out of his nose. "Is that all?"

"No, there are many more discrepancies I could point out to you, but I think you are already aware of them. I just wanted to tell you what a fool you were not to have seen the differences between the two ladies. I, myself, have only spent but a half hour in their presence and saw them," Graham gloated.

Reese was a fool. He'd noticed the differences during the house party, only refusing to admit that there were any. He'd believed what he wanted in the moment because he thought he had won the prize the night he took Evelyn to his bed. His satisfaction that he secured the foal to help his financial ruin had been his obsession. The rest was only clouds in his judgment. They obscured what his conscience tried to understand.

"I suppose now that you have your prize, you will return to neglecting your wife. I noticed her discomfort when we returned from the village."

Reese shot him a sharp look. "As I have stated before, my wife is of no concern of yours."

Graham turned serious. "That is where you are wrong. She is my sister now. I will protect Evelyn from any harm, and that includes the treatment she might suffer under your care."

"I will treat Evelyn as she deserves and nothing less," Reese snarled before he walked away.

Reese had enough of Graham's insight. How he treated his wife was his business alone. It was his right as her husband. If he chose to ignore her for their remaining married life, it was his prerogative. Reese owned Evelyn, like he owned this estate. And nothing or nobody would stop him from how he treated her. Not Graham. Not the Duke of Colebourne.

Not even Evelyn herself.

Chapter Ten

Dinner that evening was a cross between a lively affair and awkward conversation. It bounced back and forth throughout the many courses. Each time the conversation landed on Reese, the atmosphere turned uncomfortable, then someone in his family would redirect the conversation to a more enlightening subject that had the table laughing at their enjoyment.

When the subject of Charlotte and Jasper's extended stay was disclosed to Reese, it turned into an angry discussion in which Evelyn became the target who gained the full support of Reese's family.

"Should you not be continuing on with your travel? The roads to London can be most treacherous during darkness. I hope you brought enough outriders along," said Reese.

"Charlotte and Jasper have agreed to stay with us for a few days before they continue on with their journey," answered Evelyn.

"Like hell they will," Reese thundered.

Evelyn laid down the silverware and folded her hands in her lap. With her shoulders pressed back and head held high, she sat firm in her decision not to cower under Reese's anger. "They are my guests."

Reese grounded his teeth. "This is my home and I make all the decisions regarding it. And I will not tolerate them staying on."

"Then we are at a crossroads, *Lord Worthington*. Because I am adamant on their stay," said Evelyn.

"You will not defy my orders, *Lady Worthington*." Reese pounded his fist on the table.

The tableware rattled with each strike, the silverware clattering against the dishes. The table grew quiet, the guests switching their heads between each argument. Each person waited with bated breath on how the disagreement would end. Would Evelyn give into Reese's orders? Or would Evelyn stay strong with her defiance? Either way, the outcome wouldn't bode well for the couple.

Evelyn glared at Reese and then turned her head, addressing the table at large. "How shall we spend the day tomorrow?"

Maggie, the dear innocent, piped up with, "We can go fishing."

"Excellent idea, Mags," said Graham.

"I do love a day spent lazing with my pole dangling in the water, waiting for a bite," said Sinclair, arching his eyebrows at his wife.

"Jasper," hissed Charlotte, playfully slapping him on the arm.

Reese growled at his guests and family, furious they had chosen to ignore his tirade. Perhaps he needed to make himself clearer. "I have decided to accept your gift. Please, leave the paperwork for ownership before you leave this evening."

Reese threw his napkin on his chair and stalked to the door. Before he could leave, Charlotte stopped him in his tracks.

"Evelyn already holds the paperwork."

Reese turned, gritting his teeth. "Now, why would my wife hold possession of those?"

Charlotte gave him an innocent look. "Why? Because she is the owner of Cobalt."

Reese frowned, not in the mood to play games. "Do you not mean to imply that Evelyn and I are the owners?"

"No, you heard me correctly. Evelyn is the sole owner of the colt," Charlotte answered.

"You gave a gift to a woman who is spooked to death of horses? Why the very act of riding one puts her into hysterics." Reese scoffed.

"You appeared compassionate to my fear when we left the cottage," said Evelyn.

"An act, my dear *wife*. Was I very convincing? If so, I played the part well of a considerate husband protecting his wife from her fears. It does not sit well when deceived, does it?"

"I believed that you finally cared. Even though I had my doubts, I pushed them to the side to give us a chance at happiness." Evelyn threw her napkin on the table.

"A false reality. It was my plan to deceive you and trick you into believing I was somebody I was not. An act you and your sister know only so well. How does it feel to have a person you care for fool you into believing a false sense of security?"

"So our last few weeks spent as husband and wife were a means for revenge?" asked Evelyn.

"Exactly."

"You are a bastard, Worthington. You do not deserve Evelyn," snarled Charlotte.

"Nevertheless, you are aware that since Evelyn is my wife, anything she owns is now mine?" Reese directed his question at Charlotte.

"I am aware of the marriage laws. But under special circumstances, a lady can own property that her husband cannot control. Uncle Theo helped to write an iron-clad proof of ownership for this very reason."

"So, Colebourne thinks he can still control the strings?" Reese sneered.

"I suppose if you wish to state it in those terms. Yes, he does." Charlotte confirmed with a nod.

"Sinclair?" Reese asked since Sinclair had won the duke's bet.

"I agree with Charlotte and Colebourne on this matter. Also, I have no grounds to refute."

"But you won the ridiculous bet that Colebourne dangled in front of us."

"Yes, but I refused the horse. Winning Charlie's love was the only prize I desired." Sinclair kissed Charlotte's hand.

Noel sighed. "Oh, is that not the most romantic declaration you have ever heard?"

"Fool," muttered Worthington.

"A fool in love. But I am not a fool regarding the care of my sister-in-law. You have crossed the line with your disrespect toward Evelyn. I will not stand for your abuse, and I know Colebourne will stand firm in whatever decision I make on removing Evelyn from your care," declared Sinclair.

"No bother, you can have her. If you refuse to leave my home, then I will remove myself. I leave for London this evening."

"Then you will not mind if I see to Evelyn's care?" asked Graham. Graham stood and came to Evelyn's side, positioning himself as her protector. He placed a hand on her shoulder, showing Evelyn his support.

Reese gritted his teeth. "I told you to stay away from my wife."

"A threat I choose to ignore," baited Graham.

"Take your hand off of my wife," Reese growled.

Evelyn rose, squeezing Graham's hand. Then she lifted it off her shoulder and stepped forward until she reached Reese. "Shall I inform the servants of your departure?"

Reese narrowed his gaze and took in Evelyn's stance. No longer the dull miss, but a strong, defiant wife stood before him. He thought his deception would have destroyed her, but instead, she appeared stronger than ever. Were they even? If so, what now? His plan had backfired, and now his world was spinning out of control.

He looked around the table and saw how his deception caused them to view him. To Evelyn's family, he was an arrogant bastard. To his own, he had lost their love and respect if the disappointment in their gazes were anything to go by. He wanted to roar his injustice and place the blame on Evelyn. However, he was the one at fault. Evelyn had confessed her misdeeds and owned up to them. What had he done? He'd acted like a child seeking revenge.

Still, it was his fault he held onto his anger. It kept him from facing the emotions Evelyn stirred in him. He wanted to lash out with his frustrations. When Graham came behind Evelyn to wrap his arm around her waist, staking his claim, Reese chose his brother to take the burden.

Reese swung his fist back and punched Graham across the face for ignoring his threat. Brother or not, no man would ever touch Evelyn but him.

Graham might have laughed at the punch, but it didn't stop him from lunging at Reese. With another punch to Graham's middle that landed him on his knees, Reese shook out his fingers.

"I will inform them myself," Reese answered before stalking away.

~~~~~~

Evelyn watched her husband leave, conflicted with herself. Should she run after him or should she stay and help Graham? What had come over Reese? He was a contradiction. One minute, he'd spouted off to the room on how he'd played her false, then turned possessive when Graham had laid his hand on her.

She knew Graham only pretended interest in her to provoke Reese into admitting his feelings. Evelyn had overheard Graham and her mother-in-law conspiring to make Reese jealous. She had wanted to confront them, to tell them that their attempts were useless. But were they?

Graham jumped to his feet and laughed. Evelyn swung her head toward him. When she saw the twinkle in his eyes, she knew that he'd provoked Reese on purpose. She shook her head in disappointment, but that only made Graham's smile widen.

"Evelyn, you need to gather your belongings. We also leave for London tonight. I will not allow you to spend another minute under this roof. I promised Colebourne I would look after your welfare," said Sinclair.

Evelyn shook her head. "No. I will remain here. Worthington Hall is my home now."

Charlotte huffed in frustration. "You must see reason."

"I have seen reason since I followed Reese to his bed all those weeks ago. And I continue to live with it each day I am married to him."

"How? He deliberately hurt you," said Charlotte.

"No more than we deliberately deceived him when we switched identities."

Charlotte shook her head. "They are not the same."

"Are they not?" Evelyn arched an eyebrow.

"No, he deceived you for revenge. You deceived him for love," stated Charlotte.

"If you will please excuse me, I must see to my husband's departure."

"Evelyn, you need to stay scarce until Reese leaves." Graham stepped in front of Evelyn.

"Thank you for your concern. However, I am not afraid of Reese or the emotions he stirs in me."

"Evelyn?" Charlotte asked.

Evelyn sighed and addressed her sister. "Charlie, you need to understand that I love him. I explained to you before this crazy mess started how Reese made me feel and you offered your support. I need you to understand and continue supporting me. The road my marriage is traveling on is full of bumps and ruts. But it will only be until we find a smoother road to journey upon. It may take many wrong turns before we reach it, but those trials will only strengthen our marriage. And our love."

Evelyn didn't wait for any more interruptions. She needed to see Reese before he disappeared to London. She must show him her forgiveness and that she would continue to fight for their marriage. She knew he wouldn't accept her faith, but one day he would.

Evelyn stood outside Reese's bedroom door, listening to him give orders to his valet. The sharp tone of her husband's voice betrayed his firmly held temper.

His valet rushed from the room carrying a pair of boots, and he cringed when he spotted Evelyn lingering near the door. "My lady?"

"It is all right, Kemp."

The valet nodded before hustling to do his master's bidding. Evelyn slipped in between the door and closed it behind her. When the door squeaked shut, her husband lifted his head and glared, then resumed throwing items into his valise, ignoring Evelyn.

"Reese?"

He raised his head and arched his eyebrow at her familiarity. She stood tall, not letting his regard intimidate her. They were on even ground now. They had both betrayed each other. Now they could leave it all behind and start fresh. Instead of lies, they would now have the truth between them.

Evelyn started toward him and repeated herself. "Reese?"

"Madam, I see no need for your presence in my bedroom. Not only were you not invited, but if I am not mistaken, I have not given you leave to address me by my God-given name. For the remaining days of our marriage, you are to address me as Worthington."

Reese strode past Evelyn without another glance. However, he wouldn't even reach the door before his wife threw down a gauntlet.

"Does this order also stand when I whisper, moan, and scream my pleasure while you are buried deep inside me? Or can I be familiar then?"

Reese swung around, dropping his valise on the floor. He strode to Evelyn and towered over her. His anger swelled around them, wrapping them in a cloak of the forbidden. Her taunting words hung in the air. When she didn't cower from his stance and instead slid her hands down his chest, Reese growled.

"Worthington," Evelyn whispered.

Reese grabbed Evelyn around her arms, squeezing tightly, and brought her against his chest, trapping her hands. His eyes clouded with a storm that only she provoked in him. He bent his head and took her lips in a punishing kiss to frighten her away. He gave her no mercy as his mouth possessed her, displaying the fury he had barely contained at dinner.

With one arm wrapped around her, he pulled her head back and ravaged her mouth, each kiss becoming more demanding than the last. Evelyn didn't so much as whimper, but he felt her body tremble against his. She didn't tremble out of fear, but of a passion that spun out of control.

He'd lied to her belowstairs. But he must never let her know the depth of his feelings. It would give Evelyn too much power.

"Reese," Evelyn whispered.

At hearing his name on her lips, he threw her away from him. The sweet taste of her remained on his lips, tempting him with the idea of taking her before he left. He wanted to stake his claim on Evelyn and show her how little she affected him. Even though she already meant the world to him.

But he wasn't his father. He wouldn't use her, no matter how much he wanted her. He had to leave for London now. To put distance between them until he understood the pull of connection between them and decide how he would proceed with his marriage.

While in London, he would call on his mistresses and the Duke of Colebourne. He would demand his settlement and then maybe, just maybe, he might return home and make their marriage a joyful union. But until then, she needed to understand he wouldn't be biddable to her uncle. Her family thought they could play games with him. She could keep the damn horse in her name. His business in London would prove to be profitable if the information he had gained held correct.

"Worthington," he growled before striding away again.

Evelyn sighed. She thought the passion in that kiss was enough to stop Reese from leaving. The desire simmering between them had been ready to explode. Each time, it only grew stronger. Even in anger, their passion unleashed itself. He may have grabbed her in anger, but she knew that was only a thinly held façade he clung to. The day when Reese no longer denied the strength of their bond would come soon. And on that day, Evelyn would stand waiting for him with open arms. She would let him go for now, but only for a short while.

She would accept Sinclair's offer to travel to London. Evelyn planned to stake a claim on her husband's heart. Reese could run, but she wouldn't be far behind. Evelyn smiled, watching her husband leave his bedroom.

Evelyn let her gaze travel around the spacious area. She had spent many nights over the course of the last few weeks lying in his arms in this bedroom. Their lovemaking, whether intense or slow, only deepened her love for Reese. He may have always carried her back to her bed while she slept, but he no longer would on his return. With a little help from her mother-in-law, there would be a change upon her husband's return. Never would she sleep alone again. They would share a bedroom, whether or not Reese approved.

Chapter Eleven

Evelyn walked into breakfast the next morning with a spring in her step and a smile to brighten the room. She woke feeling refreshed and ready to pursue her husband.

Upon her arrival, the room fell into a hush of whispers before trailing away. All eyes were upon Evelyn, regarding her with pity. However, Evelyn would have none of that. She sat in her regular seat, spooned sugar into her tea, and took a sip. Still, the room remained quiet, each person judging her, waiting to offer any sort of sympathy toward Reese's behavior the evening before.

"Good morning, family."

Each person murmured a greeting, then pretended to find interest in their food.

Evelyn smiled while buttering a scone. "I miss our morning ritual."

Charlie stared curiously at Evelyn's joyous manner. "I do too. On some mornings, I ride over and join them."

"Mmm, perhaps I will make a visit in the early morning hours during my trip to London."

"Then you agree to allow me to take you away from here?" asked Sinclair.

"No. You may provide me with transportation to London. Once we arrive, I shall join my husband at his residence. He has a residence, does he not?" Evelyn turned toward Graham.

"He does." Graham smiled.

"Excellent. When do you wish to depart?"

"How soon do you wish to join your husband?" asked Sinclair.

"Well, I wish to join him as soon as possible. But with the snit he was in, perhaps I will give him two days to settle his temper." Evelyn bit into the scone.

"Three," Eden coughed behind her napkin.

"Three?" Evelyn raised her eyebrows.

Every member of Reese's family nodded in agreement.

"Then three days from now we shall depart. I have a few changes I need to put in motion before I leave. So, the extra day will fall in perfectly with my plans. Since Reese took off without seeing to the care of Cobalt, Graham, can you please confer with Sinclair and the stable master on the horse's care?"

"Yes. And if the Sinclair's would not mind another passenger, I would love to travel to London with your party. That way, I can help you settle into your London residence," said Graham.

"An excellent idea. We'd love your company," answered Evelyn.

Soon, the table erupted in mindless chatter about Evelyn's trip to London. Reese's family seemed relieved that Evelyn hadn't sunk into a depression from Reese's unpredictable behavior. Instead, Evelyn couldn't be happier. Her plan had come together easier than she thought. She had hoped that Graham would offer to accompany them to London. A devious smile lit her face.

When her gaze landed on Charlie, her sister narrowed her eyes at Evelyn. Evelyn smiled innocently at Charlie, but that didn't fool her sister. No, Charlie knew Evelyn better than Evelyn knew herself, if not better.

Charlie mouthed, "We will talk," and Evelyn continued smiling with a quick nod.

Eden, Noel, and Maggie left breakfast to take up their studies in the library. Charlie rose with Sinclair and Graham to make arrangements for Cobalt's care. Evelyn promised Charlie a walk in the gardens later. That left Evelyn alone with Lady Worthington at the table.

"My dear, there is much I wish to apologize to you for, but I do not know where to begin." Lady Worthington sighed heavily. "My son's behavior was deplorable. Ever since his father died, his control has slipped from his grasp, leaving you with the burden of his outlandish behavior. If you desire to return to your uncle's home, no one in this family would lay the blame at your feet."

Evelyn reached across the table for her mother-in-law's hand. "Mama, I have no intention of ever leaving Reese." Evelyn smiled wickedly.

Lady Worthington's expression grew warm at Evelyn's endearment. Evelyn spoke the truth when she called Lady Worthington "Mama." Ever since her arrival, the lady had made her a part of their family, never once judging Evelyn for her past actions, nor had the lady portrayed any sign of reluctance on passing the countess duties over to Evelyn.

Evelyn hadn't changed how the household ran. She only added soft touches to make it her own. She respected Lady Worthington too much to hurt her feelings, not when she loved the lady as she would have loved her own mother. Evelyn missed the gentle guidance of an older woman. While Aunt Susanna had been a comfort over the years and embraced all the girls as her own, she hadn't been a constant companion.

Lady Worthington sighed her relief and squeezed Evelyn's hand. "Do you know how comforting your words are?"

"I am the one who seeks your forgiveness. I now understand the depth of my deception with your son. In time, I only hope he will forgive me. I will not give up on him. In fact, I plan to pursue your son and seduce him into submission." Evelyn laughed.

Lady Worthington joined Evelyn's laughter. "How may I be of assistance?"

"While I am away in London, I need your help in moving my belongings into Reese's bedroom. I will no longer stand for a marriage of convenience or separation. Reese will no longer use me to his advantage whenever he feels the urge. On our return from London, our marriage will be a loving union."

Lady Worthington inclined her head. "It will be my pleasure."

Evelyn's smile grew wider at her mother-in-law's agreement to assist in seducing her husband. They spent the next hour with Evelyn describing how she wanted their room decorated upon their return and Evelyn's other requirements for the home.

In return, Lady Worthington explained Reese's moods and how to work around them. She also explained their home in London and promised to write to the butler and housekeeper to warn them of her arrival and to keep it a secret from Reese. When Evelyn questioned their loyalty, Lady Worthington laughed and explained how the servants did her biddings, not Reese's. She described how Reese never cared for the instructions with the servants and kept the responsibility with his mother. Horses were Reese's primary obsession. Everything else besides the responsibilities of his title held no interest with Reese.

Once they finished their discussion, Evelyn followed Lady Worthington into the library to visit with her new sisters before her walk with Charlie. Reese's sisters were amusing to spend time with, and she would miss them while she was away in London. Never once had they shown her anything but love. Even more so when Reese acted like a brute. For a short while, he had been the most amorous, attentive husband a woman could ask for. Eden and Noel bombarded her with advice on how to handle Reese.

Maggie had everyone in a fit of laughter when she told Evelyn the way to make Reese smitten with her. Evelyn only needed to sit on a horse and ride around in circles in front of him.

While her comment held an enormous amount of truth to it, it was the one thing Evelyn would never do. Her fear of horses kept her from being anywhere near them. But could Evelyn put her fear aside to show Reese her commitment to their marriage? Could she attempt to find common ground with her husband?

Another idea formed. Charlie was the only person she trusted to help her with her fear. She would have preferred her husband's guidance, but if she wanted to prove the depth of her love to him, then what better way than to show him she no longer feared horses?

~~~~~~

Evelyn and Charlie walked amongst the blooms with their arms interlocked. Neither of them had spoken. Evelyn was still lost in her thoughts on how to seduce Reese once she reached London. This time, she wouldn't use deceit. She would use determination to make her husband understand that what they shared was rare and a once-in-a-lifetime feeling. And if he was too dense to see it for himself, then Evelyn would use every opportunity to prove they needed to cherish the love they held for one another. For some reason, the connection between them frightened her husband.

Evelyn knew the fear came from watching his own parent's marriage. His father had been bent on destroying his mother. At every opportunity, the late earl had flaunted his mistresses in front of Lady Worthington and demeaned every word she spoke. Evelyn knew Lady Worthington held no love for her late husband, but relief that she no longer had to endure their marriage and her children wouldn't be under his rule and ridicule.

Anyone could tell the Worthington children demonstrated the upbringing of a loving parent, a woman who cherished them with all her heart and had guided them into the amazing souls they were. While Reese had been under his father's hand more than the other children, Lady Worthington's guidance still held strong in his character.

Reese might have had to spend more time with his elder to learn how to rule the earldom one day, but it was his mother's character that held strong in Reese. From his sense of humor to his gentle care of the ones he loved.

Evelyn also understood the pressure Reese had taken on upon his father's death. He'd poured his heart and soul into a breeding program for horses that challenged the most experienced horseman. Because his father had gambled and whored away the family coffers, he stood to have it taken away at any moment. To put it bluntly, the Worthingtons were on the edge of financial ruin.

Reese had tried any solution to keep their family afloat by hanging onto the edge with his fingertips. When Uncle Theo dangled an offer at Reese, her husband had grabbed ahold to secure his family. Only because of Evelyn's selfishness to make Reese hers, he'd lost the chance for survival. Or so he thought. Instead of realizing what he gained, he had stubbornly denied what could make his life richer.

Oh, Evelyn was no fool. She understood the world they lived in. The more money one had, the more power they held. Reese may be an earl, but he was a penniless one. Few knew the truth yet, but it didn't matter. It only took one person to know for the rest of the ton to learn of Reese's financial ruin. His rank would be the only reason his family would continue to receive invitations.

However, once the merchants learned the state of his financial affairs, accounts would be closed. Even with his marriage to Evelyn, the ton could still shun Reese. Especially if the Duke of Colebourne didn't offer his support of the marriage.

Even though Uncle Theo knew Evelyn loved Reese, it wouldn't be enough if Reese didn't express his love for Evelyn for Uncle Theo to see. And so far, her husband had done nothing to prove otherwise. In fact, his actions kept showing the complete opposite. Once they reached London, her uncle would learn of Reese's latest bout of temper.

While she could convince Charlie to stay quiet, Sinclair was another matter. Sinclair didn't approve of Reese's treatment and would find pleasure in informing her uncle of Reese's cruel words. Evelyn hoped to convince Charlie to sweet-talk Sinclair into staying silent, at least until Evelyn could make Reese believe in their love. A small feat by no means.

"I can hear your wheels spinning, sister. Spill," ordered Charlie.

"Is it making you tired?" Evelyn joked over their shared secret.

Charlie pretended to sigh dramatically. "Tremendously. I never slept a wink last night once Jasper—"

Evelyn covered her ears. "Please, keep your intimate moments to yourself."

Charlie laughed. "You never even let me finish."

"Nor will I. The words night and Jasper combined is enough to leave me with nightmares." Evelyn shuddered.

"The act of my husband loving me leaves you with terrors?" Charlie gasped for effect. However, her smile gave her away.

"Your husband may love you to his heart's desire. However, I have no wish to learn of the details."

"Well, for your information, because of your husband's display of a tantrum, my husband did not display his love." Charlie shot her a dirty look Evelyn knew she didn't mean. "Instead he spent the night pacing the rug with anger at your husband's idiocy. Jasper is not a fan of Worthington's from his attempts to win my hand at the house party. Then, Worthington made his standing worse when he spoke so insincerely in his regards to you once he discovered our deception. However, I convinced Jasper how much you loved him and to look at Worthington in a new light, especially after your recent letters where you wrote of his devotion. We thought he had changed, but apparently not. No, my dear sister, I spent the entire evening calming Jasper. My husband wants to remove you from Worthington's care, and after witnessing Worthington's disregard, I support Jasper's decision."

Evelyn patted Charlie's hand, pulling away and sitting on a bench. She patted the spot next to her, but Charlie declined. Instead, her sister paced back and forth, detailing why Evelyn should leave Reese. Evelyn looked upon Charlie with humor and let her mind wander.

For the first time in a long while, Evelyn felt at peace with herself. She had broken out of her shell to live, and it felt invigorating. No, the circumstances weren't the best, and her marriage hung in limbo, but Evelyn had never felt more alive. Her excitement with her plans for Reese was barely contained. She continued to let Charlie rant, for that was how her sister operated. Once Charlie settled, Evelyn would share her plans.

"Uncle Theo wants you to move back in with him, but Sinclair and I both agreed that you should stay with us," Charlie said, bringing Evelyn out of her thoughts.

Evelyn shook her head. "Your offer is very kind. However, my place is beside my husband."

Charlie huffed. "Have you not listened to a word I said?"

In truth, Evelyn hadn't. She'd become lost in her own musings. Evelyn had heard bits and pieces and come to the conclusion that Charlie's rant was all the negative aspects of Reese. But those traits were what drew Evelyn to Reese. They were what made him the gentleman he was. Yes, he had flaws, but she loved every one of them.

Charlie threw her hands in the air, frustrated with Evelyn. Which only caused Evelyn to smile more. When Charlie growled, Evelyn knew she needed to calm Charlie before her sister took off and did something foolish. Charlie had the tendency to act out before she thought.

Evelyn offered the seat next to her again, and this time Charlie collapsed on the bench. "I admit, I may not have been listening to your tirade, but I get the full impact of your words. You wish for me to abandon my husband and the love I hold for him. To treat him in the same regard his own father used to. No. I will not destroy the bond that holds us. It might be a fragile string with each strand fraying away, but it still binds us to one another. I only ask for your support while I repair those pieces into the hold that it is meant to be."

"We made a mess of things with our deception," said Charlie.

"Yes. My husband holds strong in trust, and I deceived him with my actions. I see that now. To him, I showed that I couldn't be trusted in the same way his father never could be."

"I am sorry for the part I played. I only wished for your happiness." Charlie reached for Evelyn's hand.

"You only went along with my wishes. I should never have played the risk. I wish I had been more forward and declared my interest. Only, I let my shyness and reserved character hold me back. Except when I pretended to be you, I was able to let it all disappear and become the young girl I used to be when Mama and Papa were alive. And for that, I only have myself to blame."

Each sister sat silent, lost in their thoughts of a simpler time when their parents were alive. Evelyn had embraced life in the same manner as Charlie. Even though Charlie pushed the boundaries after their parents died, she had continued to live life to the fullest, while Evelyn had cocooned herself away into a shell, living in fear of losing again. Through the years she didn't realize that she had lost again. Evelyn lost herself. She lost the ability to live a carefree life. If she didn't take action now, she would lose Reese too.

"So, Lady Worthington, what are your plans for Lord Worthington?"

Evelyn laughed at Charlie's attempt at humor. "Why, Lady Sinclair, once I reach London, I shall pursue Lord Worthington with a seduction that will have him once again falling to his knees at my feet."

"A feat I know you will accomplish with the determination you hold in your eyes. It will be no small act, but one he will fall victim to in the end. I only hope for your case that when he falls into the abyss he clings to you tightly, never letting go."

"I hope so, too," Evelyn whispered. "In which, I will need your help once we reach London with a small favor."

Charlie's eyes lit up with excitement that she could aid her sister in winning her husband's hand. "With pleasure."

Chapter Twelve

Graham sat across from Evelyn, his gaze darting back and forth between her and Charlie. During the last hour of their carriage ride, he had been doing this. At times he would humph, or his lips would twist in thought or his head would tilt from side to side as he judged them. He must have thought no one took notice of his regard.

Especially with Sinclair and Charlie in a heated debate on the merits of the livestock they wanted to purchase for their breeding program. Her sister held different opinions than her husband on the quality of horseflesh each required. Charlie remained stubborn and kept threatening Sinclair on returning to work at Uncle Theo's estate. To that, Sinclair pretended indifference and baited Charlie with his own taunts.

Evelyn shook her head. Even though their marriage held strong in love, it still didn't stop them from falling back into their old behavior.

Evelyn tuned them out and tried to concentrate on her book, but Graham's open perusal drew her curiosity. Oh, she knew that before long, Graham would state his observations. He was a lot like Charlie in that regard, never keeping his thoughts to himself. He wanted to observe people's reactions to his blunt remarks. So she pretended indifference, letting Graham process his thoughts. She hoped that was his intention, so when he spoke, it wouldn't cause everyone in the carriage too much discomfort. For there was nowhere to disappear to while stuck in a carriage.

"Mmm," said Graham.

Evelyn closed her book, leaving her fingers in between the pages she had been trying to read. She might as well stop trying because her thoughts consumed her with wondering how Reese would react once he discovered her invasion into his life. Did he return to his mistresses' arms? Evelyn had heard the rumors of Reese's pursuits when he visited London. Charlie had confirmed them from Sinclair's rants. Would Reese continue in his father's footsteps with lovers, drink, and gambling? She knew he held no funds for gambling, but like many lords in London, he could wager with no funds once he obtained credit. Many gentlemen loaned money and held the vowels with the intention of wiping them away for a favor here or there.

There were many thoughts rambling in her head that she feared. However, they wouldn't keep her from her goal.

Soon, Graham's musing drew Sinclair's and Charlie's attention too. Their conversation ceased, and Charlie tilted her head at Graham, like she did when something or someone drew her curiosity.

"Fool," Graham muttered again.

"Are you calling my sister a fool?" Charlie growled, sitting forward in the seat.

"No, my brother." Graham held up his hand in defense.

"Yes. On that I will agree with you," said Charlie, relaxing back against the cushions.

"I second," said Sinclair.

Evelyn never broke her gaze from Graham. She knew he wanted her to agree with them. However, she refused to. Because she was the fool, not Reese.

"Do you not agree?" asked Graham.

"No, I do not," answered Evelyn, folding her hands on top of her book.

"Mmm, interesting," said Graham.

"How so?" asked Evelyn.

"Do you agree that he is at least blind?" asked Graham, evading Evelyn's question.

"I kept questioning his blindness throughout the house party," declared Sinclair.

"It is more than obvious," said Graham.

Sinclair nodded. "Exactly."

Evelyn and Charlie exchanged glances, then shrugged their confusion at Graham and Sinclair's conversation. What were her brothers-in-law stating?

"Their eyes," stated Graham.

"Their smiles," said Sinclair.

"Their laughter."

"Their temper."

The gentlemen continued to compare the differences between Evelyn and Charlie. Their argument stated that while they looked the same, they were the complete opposites in character. And anyone who interacted with them should notice they were two entirely different ladies.

"To defend Worthington, they went to elaborate ends to confuse him," said Sinclair.

Graham turned his head toward Sinclair. "Oh? How so?"

"Well, they had me confused the first time they changed clothes at the house party and switched their identities. And I have known them their entire lives. If Charlie did not display a few clues, I would not have noticed myself."

"However, you did?" asked Graham.

"Yes." Jasper smiled wickedly at Charlie.

"How else did they confuse him?"

"They would wear the same color of dress and arrange their hair the same. They went so far to switch places right under his nose, and still, Worthington was clueless." Sinclair shook his head in disgust.

"Still, every single nuance of them is different," Graham emphasized.

"Yes. I am afraid your brother's attention was more focused on what he would gain instead of the actual prize," said Sinclair.

"Well, if it is any consolation, dear Evelyn, I informed my brother shortly after you arrived that he was a fool not to have noted the difference. For I know I would have immediately."

"Thank you." Evelyn smiled brightly.

"So what are your devious plans for my unsuspecting brother, and how may I be of assistance?" Graham asked, rubbing his hands together.

"I think it would be best if I do not make you privy to any plans I have formulating."

Graham gasped with a twinkling smile. "Where is the fun in that?"

"I do not wish to cause discord in our family. And with your attempts at making Reese jealous, you only make him furious."

"Ahh, but he is so much more fun when he is in a snit." Graham laughed.

Evelyn's eyes narrowed on Graham. "You take pleasure from antagonizing him." It wasn't a question she asked, but a realization she now understood.

"Sometimes it is the only way for Reese to see what is before his eyes. It may take him a while to process his foolishness, but in the end, he always does."

"Still, while I appreciate your help, I think you should stop your flirtation and treat me as one of your sisters."

Graham moaned good-naturedly. "You two are perfect for one another. Neither of you will allow me any fun. However, since I love you already like a dear sister, I will offer my support however you deem necessary."

Evelyn nodded. "Can you explain to us how you can tell me and Charlie apart when Reese cannot? I understand how Sinclair can since he has known us forever."

"While both of you are identical in appearance, and both lovely I might add, you each carry yourselves differently."

"How so?" Charlie asked.

Graham looked to Sinclair for help. He didn't want to offend either lady. They were both stunning in comparison, but Evelyn held a certain grace her sister didn't. Not that Charlotte Sinclair wasn't graceful, only … Oh, Graham had once again spoken before he processed his thoughts.

Sinclair shrugged, letting him know that Graham had started it and he would be of no help. Graham opened his eyes wider, shocked that Sinclair wouldn't help him smooth this into a more acceptable explanation. Instead, Sinclair only laughed.

"Well … you both …" Graham tried to start.

"We both what?" Charlie's tone turned offensive.

"Yes, what do we both?" asked Evelyn, her curiosity shining in her eyes. If Graham wasn't mistaken, he also spied a hint of mischief twinkling.

"Well, your eyes …"

"Are both green," said Charlie.

"Yes, but Charlie has gold that flecks and Evelyn's eyes hold a silver sparkle," explained Graham.

"You noticed that?" asked Evelyn. "But Reese didn't."

"What else?" Charlie demanded.

"Um, you each carry a unique fragrance. Yes, that is it. Charlie, you smell like chocolate for some reason. And, Evelyn, whenever you are in a room, I catch a scent of raspberries and vanilla."

Graham thought he was in the clear by referencing two distinct similarities that wouldn't offend them. However, each lady sat waiting for him to spill more. Which he refused to do. He might be as foolish as his brother, but he wouldn't place himself in a situation where either lady would take offense at the differences that were more than obvious. They still had another day of traveling before they reached London, and he didn't want to ride in a carriage with two ladies whose feelings he might hurt if he spoke the truth. So, instead, his gaze darted around the carriage while trying not to make eye contact with either lady.

He glanced out the window. "We are having excellent weather for this journey."

The carriage erupted in laughter from the two sisters. Graham's gaze swung to them. They stared at him, laughing at his uncomfortableness. This was a side of Evelyn he had never seen before. Sure, he had watched her find enjoyment with his family, but never the silliness she displayed with her sister. He wondered if Reese could stay immune to this side of Evelyn. For if he could, he was more foolish than Graham thought. Evelyn looked downright adorable with her cheeks rosy, laughter dancing in her eyes, and silly giggles spilling from her opened mouth.

"Shall we put him out of his misery?" Evelyn asked.

Charlie laughed. "I suppose we can. Even though it is much more fun to watch him squirm."

"So true, but he has endeared himself to me with his support."

"Very well," said Charlie.

Evelyn reached across the carriage and patted Graham's knee before sitting back in the seat. At every attempt, she tried to bring her laughter under control, but then Charlie would start laughing harder, and Evelyn fell into another gaggle of giggles again. Even Sinclair joined in, leaving Graham left out of their humor.

Once Evelyn controlled herself with deep breaths, she smiled serenely at him before confessing, "We apologize for our attempt to play innocent to your discomfort. Charlie and I both know how completely opposite we are from one another. While only our family members will point out the differences, it was refreshing for someone who has not known us our entire lives to see the discrepancies. In our foolishness, we were hoping you would show your bravery by telling us."

Graham nodded at his understanding. He thought to make them suffer for a brief spell for making him uncomfortable. "I can see where my brother did not appreciate your attempts to fool him."

The carriage grew silent, and the ladies appeared scolded by their antics.

"However, I so graciously do. Very well, heathens, you had me completely fooled and smitten." Graham laughed.

The carriage roared with laughter at the humor of the delicate situation, and Graham offered his support to Evelyn for whatever she had planned. For the rest of the carriage ride, they made arrangements for when they reached London. They decided to drop Graham and Evelyn off first at Worthington's townhome in Mayfair once they arrived. Then Evelyn made plans with Charlie for the following day to visit their family at the Colebourne house in St. James.

Evelyn's anticipation grew each mile they traveled closer to London. She wondered what Reese was doing at that exact moment. Once they arrived, would he be at home? With much impatience, Evelyn had to wait another day before discovering her husband's pastimes.

Chapter Thirteen

While Evelyn wondered of Reese's pastimes, Reese sat debating whether he should remain in London or return home to his wife.

He missed Evelyn something fiercely. Once his temper had calmed and he rationally thought over the course of his actions, he finally saw them for what they were: a tantrum. He'd acted like a four-year-old child in his treatment of Evelyn. He tried to forget how he hurt her with his deception, but he couldn't remove the heaviness that weighed on his conscience no matter how hard he tried to rationalize it. The matter of it, plain and simple, was that he had been a fool since the first time he kissed Evelyn. Making one foolish mistake after another.

Every time he closed his eyes, he saw the pain reflected in Evelyn's gaze. Even though she'd taunted him with her desire before he left, he'd still caused her pain by rejecting her yet again. His brother stood correct in that he had changed into the very image of his bastard of a father. With each instance of him unleashing his fury with Evelyn, his father's tarnished hand rose behind it. Every kiss, every caress, filled with revenge.

Except his revenge had backfired. Evelyn had invaded his soul and clung to him, never releasing her hold. Did he even want her to? He didn't know. Either way, he needed to make amends. Only, he didn't hold a clue if she would accept them.

Before her family arrived, Reese had almost fooled himself into believing their marriage was real. While he fooled Evelyn, he had been no different. Every kiss from her enflamed his senses. Every caress made him ache for more. Every time Evelyn screamed her pleasure, Reese craved to hear the sound again. They had settled into marital bliss, and Reese had finally found contentment.

And he tossed that peaceful marriage away because Evelyn had tricked his ego and wounded his pride. All because she loved him. Him. Evelyn had fallen in love with a man Reese didn't even know existed.

Reese swallowed a long slug from the bottle of whiskey held in his grip, a hold he hadn't relinquished for the past two hours. He slid lower in his chair, propping his feet on the ottoman, and stared into the blazing hearth. Images of his wife danced before him in the flames. Evelyn laughing while he tickled her. Evelyn gazing at him in adoration. Evelyn dancing in his arms. Evelyn making love with him.

At each lick of the flames, another image appeared. With each image, he took another swig from the bottle until it was empty. He dropped the container and listened to it clink against the other empty bottle he had drunk.

His eyes grew heavy, sleep beckoning. The temptation to slumber sounded ideal. However, he knew that once he succumbed, Evelyn would float in and out of his subconscious. Each time would be different. Reese never wanted to open his eyes when his dreams turned tantalizing, but when they turned to nightmares of Evelyn's pain, he woke drenched in sweat. Would she ever forgive him?

A clatter in the hallway disturbed Reese, but he knew Rogers would reprimand the servants. He'd hired the butler at his London residence himself after firing his father's insubordinate servants upon his death. None of them respected Reese as the new earl and defied every single one of his wishes. So, Reese had fired the lot and employed Rogers, who had hired a whole new staff.

Since Reese arrived at his London residence, the progress the staff had made pleased him. That was, until now. However, he wouldn't take his fury out on them. They weren't to blame. He only had himself to hold accountable for becoming drunk in the middle of the afternoon when he should have been at his club learning about the next auction at Tattersalls and the horseflesh on display. Instead, he was sulking like a pitiful fool, feeling sorry for himself.

The house grew silent for a brief minute before changing to a roar of activity. Servants clattered down the staircase, Rogers shouted orders, and friendly chatter echoed along the hallway. Then Reese heard the tinkling laughter of a lady.

Not any lady. But his wife. Evelyn.

Reese lurched from the chair and stumbled to the door. He wrenched it open and attempted to stride down the hallway to the foyer, but with every step, his uneven balance tripped his feet. He bounced against the walls, jostled the tables, and saw two of everything. However, once he reached the end of his destination, he only saw one of her. Only one Evelyn stood radiant against the open doorway, the rays of the sun casting an aura around her. Amazing. Graham was introducing her to Rogers, and they laughed at a joke, with Evelyn pressing her hand against Graham's arm.

"I see you did not take heed to my warning," Reese slurred.

Evelyn and Graham turned in astonishment at Reese's appearance. They appeared surprised that he would be in residence. Did they think to start an affair under his roof? Graham's expression swiftly changed to enjoyment at seeing his brother in a drunken state, while Evelyn's turned to concern. However, she didn't fool him. No, sir. Reese now understood his wife and how she deceived others. Well, no more.

"On the contrary, no. However, my lovely sister-in-law requested that I do. So to please her, I shall no longer burden Evelyn with my flirtation skills."

Reese watched Evelyn smile at Graham as they shared a special secret Reese would never be privy to. This only fueled the flames of jealousy sparking inside of Reese.

"Hmm, so instead my wife plans to flaunt your devotion to her in my face. As if I would care."

Evelyn gasped. Reese left her speechless. It appeared as if her husband was well into the bottle, with his red-rimmed eyes, disheveled appearance, slurred words, and unsteadiness. Evelyn had thought that perhaps Reese might have calmed enough for them to discuss their marriage, but his insults proved otherwise.

Reese waved his arm, stumbling. "However, I will not allow for such an affair to happen under my roof. If you desire a taste of my wife, you will need to find your own residence. Also, you have my permission, even though I did not know you liked my seconds. However, you will find nothing disappointing with the lovely Evelyn. She tastes most divine."

Evelyn paled at his words. From where he stood, he watched her body shake. From anger or shame, he didn't know. He only knew that, in his drunken state, he had whored his wife out to his brother with his permission in front of the servants, not to mention her family standing on the front stoop.

If his gut had suffered remorse before, it was nothing compared to the sense of doom that shook his body now. Shame flooded him, and he stood motionless regarding the scene folding out before him. It was as if he were in another dimension, watching a scene from afar instead of the one happening before him.

"Rogers, if you could please show me to my room." Evelyn spoke coldly, but with a dignity that only Evelyn held.

Rogers, uncomfortable with the family drama, escorted Evelyn up the stairs that led to the bedroom. When she swept past him, she wouldn't meet his gaze. Her lips trembled and Reese saw tears clinging to her lashes. With one blink, they would have rushed along her cheeks, but she kept her gaze focused ahead and avoided him. He reached out for her, but his arm hung in mid-air, his fingers stretching but unable to grasp Evelyn.

However, her sister wouldn't show the same grace. She followed behind Evelyn and stopped in front of him. Charlotte snarled at him her dislike, and in his intoxicated state, he realized the differences. He stared at Charlotte and felt not an ounce of emotion. Yet, when he watched his wife walk away, the love he held for Evelyn came to a crashing halt. He loved her, and because of his stupidity, he'd ruined his chance with her. All because of his jealousy at the affection Evelyn shared with Graham.

"Bastard," Charlotte hissed before slapping Reese across the face.

With Sinclair, Reese wouldn't be so lucky. Sinclair stalked over the threshold, rushing at Reese with a fury most deserved. Sinclair grabbed Reese by his shirt and yanked him forward. When Reese stayed at home to drink his emotions away, he'd discarded his suit coat, cravat, and waistcoat. He'd even undone a few buttons.

"Bastard is too kind of a word, my love, for this pile of shite," Sinclair bit out. "Gather Evelyn. She is coming home with us. I will not allow her to spend another moment under this arse's roof."

Charlotte didn't wait for any more instructions. She scrambled up the stairs in search of her sister. Worthington waited for the brutality Sinclair kept tightly controlled, expecting a pummeling. Except it never came. As quickly as Sinclair grabbed a hold of him, he pushed Worthington away.

Sinclair wiped his hands along his suit coat. "You are not worth the effort to sully my hands."

However, his brother wouldn't show such kindness. Once Sinclair stepped away and followed his wife up the stairs to gather Evelyn, Graham stepped forward. Before Reese could defend himself, Graham repaid Reese for his brutal treatment earlier in the week. Graham cocked his arm back and shot it forward. His fist caught Reese square in the eye.

Reese swore as pain blasted his face. He couldn't say he didn't deserve it, but it hurt more than he cared to admit.

Before he could gather his bearings, Graham's other arm shot upward into Reese's gut. Reese doubled over with a wheeze.

Just for good measure, Graham added an extra punch to Reese's other eye, knocking him back against the wall. As the air rushed out of him, Reese slid onto the floor and tipped over.

"You're a fool, brother," he vaguely heard Graham tell him.

Between the amount of alcohol he'd consumed and Graham's brutal fists, Reese saw the twinkling of stars that matched Evelyn's eyes before he passed out in a sprawl across the hallway.

Graham shook his fingers out and looked down at his brother in disgust. He was ashamed to call Reese his brother after watching him ruin Evelyn with his slanderous words. He sighed and hung his head, wondering how he could fix his brother's blunder. From the reeking stench of alcohol in the air, his brother wasn't just a fool, but a drunken fool.

Graham kicked his foot out to nudge Reese, but his brother only sprawled his body out more across the hall, and a loud snore escaped his lips. Graham searched for a servant to help him carry his brother to his bed, but there were none to be found. Of course not. Reese had made everyone so bloody uncomfortable with his accusations that everyone had made themselves scarce.

Graham prayed none of the servants would judge Evelyn too harshly. Lord knew she risked her heart enough by chasing after Reese. But for her own husband to degrade her in front of the servants by suggesting she was loose with her favors? It was too much for any lady. He hoped the new servants his brother hired after their father passed would stay loyal to their family. However, Graham knew that wouldn't be the case. It was not how the hierarchy of servants worked, especially newly hired servants. Rumors would spread like wildfire. Before Evelyn even entered society, gossip would spread of her loose morals. It wouldn't even matter that the Duke of Colebourne was her uncle.

Reese had ruined Evelyn in more ways than one.

Graham raised his head at the footsteps coming down the stairs. Sinclair stomped down them, looking for a fight. Charlotte followed him a few steps behind.

"Evelyn?" Graham asked.

"She refuses to come home with us. Evelyn stated that she made this journey for a reconciliation, and she will see it through to the end. No matter the circumstances," Sinclair growled.

Graham nodded in understanding. He admired Evelyn's bravery to fight against Reese's stubbornness. He just didn't know if his brother was worth it. He feared it was too late. The man lying on the floor reminded him of his father, a worthless bastard with a heart of stone. Graham didn't even think Evelyn could crack Reese.

"I tried to reason with her, but when Evelyn sets her heart on something, no one can change her mind. And she has her heart set on this lump." Charlotte kicked her leg out, landing it in Reese's side.

It had no effect on Reese. He continued snoring, oblivious to the scandal he'd created.

Graham sighed in disgust. "Can you at least help me carry him to his bed before you leave? All the servants have made themselves scarce."

"He deserves to lie on the floor," Sinclair snarled.

"I agree. But please, think of Evelyn. He has already caused her enough embarrassment. I do not want her to see him in this state," said Graham.

After a moment, Sinclair finally relented, though he looked just as reluctant. "All right."

Graham and Sinclair carried Reese up the stairs to his bed. Along the way, Sinclair *accidentally* lost his hold on Reese a few times, causing him to either knock his head on the railing or against the wall. Graham knew Sinclair did it on purpose by his smirks. Maybe his brother deserved it. Once in Reese's room, they threw him on his bed, and he landed near the edge.

Before Sinclair reached the door, he turned back and glared at Graham. "I am leaving her under your care. I will send a carriage for Evelyn in the morning to accompany Charlotte to visit her family. You better make sure your brother keeps his distance from Evelyn. I will pay a visit to the Duke of Colebourne this evening to update him on their marriage. Between our visit to your home and his slander of Evelyn's character, hold no surprise on the outcome of the duke's wrath. Your brother walked a thin line to begin with. Now he is hanging off a cliff where his enemies gather, waiting to peel each finger away until there is nothing to keep him from falling."

Graham understood the message behind Sinclair's words. The duke had given his niece time to make her marriage work. However, after he heard the full story of Reese's treatment, the duke himself would seek his own source of retribution. One that would leave their family destroyed. Colebourne won't leave Reese as a casualty, but ruined beyond repair. Not even Evelyn's love could save him.

Graham shoved Reese into the middle of the bed so the fool didn't fall off. His brother would be sore enough come morning. He looked at the bruises around Reese's eyes and smiled smugly. He deserved worse, but at least Graham received some satisfaction from putting his brother in his place. Graham turned and left, not even bothering to cover Reese. His brother didn't deserve any comfort. Reese only deserved a miserable existence.

Graham paused at the room next door to Reese, trying to decide if he should knock. What would he say? He refused to apologize for Reese's behavior. No, his brother would have to do his own groveling. His heart went out to Evelyn and the trials her marriage had brought to her. Still, he admired her determination to make Reese appreciate the love they shared. He only hoped his brother realized it before it was too late.

Graham continued to his room. Evelyn had dealt with enough Worthington gentlemen today. He didn't need to keep reminding her of the bloke lying oblivious to his foolishness next door.

~~~~~~

Evelyn waited for the house to grow quiet before she opened the door that led into her husband's bedroom. The servants had carried in her luggage, and Rogers had introduced Evelyn to Sally, a maid who would see to her care during her stay in London.

At first, the servants had refused to meet her eyes, but when Evelyn asked them questions on the routine of the house and hid her own embarrassment, they soon talked openly, offering her kindness. Aunt Susanna had been very informative when she prepared the girls for marriage. She told them there would be instances when their husbands would make complete arses out of themselves in front of the servants and how they were to behave. They should never allow the servants to see how the outburst affected them. They were to remain indifferent, even though they seethed with rage or wept on the inside.

So Evelyn took the advice and put everyone at ease. When Graham knocked on her door, he didn't bring up the scene from when they arrived, but saw to her care. She declined to eat dinner with him, pleading exhaustion. Instead, she ate dinner in her room, placed her belongings into their proper places, and waited for darkness to settle. Evelyn heard Graham return to his room and retire for the evening.

When her own lids started drifting shut, she shook herself awake and pressed her ear against the door. She hadn't heard a sound from her husband since he'd offered her so willingly to Graham. Sinclair had told her how Graham had knocked Reese unconscious. Fool that Evelyn was, she only wanted to offer comfort to her husband and to see to his wounds, but she knew she couldn't show her weakness to Graham, Charlie, Sinclair, or to the servants. Everyone must see her strength to believe in her ability to bring Reese to his knees. She knew her husband had felt remorse as soon as the words left his mouth. While they had shocked her, she also noticed he regretted them deeply.

Evelyn cracked the door open slowly, waiting for it to creak. When there was no sound, she opened it wide enough to slip through. The servants had lit a fire for Reese but had left him sleeping in his clothes. His light snores echoed in the quiet room. Evelyn stood over him, gazing down at her bedraggled husband sleeping peacefully like a child. Innocent. In which he was everything but that one word. There were many words she could think of in her vocabulary to describe her husband, and none of them were as kind as innocent.

Evelyn slid off Reese's footwear and undid the buttons on the placket of his trousers. When Reese shifted on the bed, muttering in his sleep, she pulled back, afraid she had woken him. Once he settled back down, she breathed a sigh of relief. She wouldn't take the chance to pull his pants off. Instead, she covered him with a light blanket. Then she lit a candle near his bedside and sat on the edge of the bed.

She noted the bruises covering his eyes and tenderly reached out to caress them away. Reese sighed in his sleep at her touch. When he didn't awaken, Evelyn kept tracing her fingers across his face, easing his pain. The soft bristles covering his cheeks scraped against her soft palm.

Evelyn's heart ached. Not for herself, but for Reese. Their marriage had been a whirlwind in which he had never found his footing. While she understood his misery, she hadn't forgiven him for his cruelty. No, even she had her pride. She had come to London to pursue her husband and seduce him into admitting his love for her.

Instead, she would now make her husband pursue her if he wanted their marriage. If Reese didn't make amends for his actions, then Evelyn would make Reese realize what he had lost. After all, she was a Holbrooke, and Holbrookes were not quitters.

Evelyn slipped under the covers and snuggled against Reese. She was cold and only he could warm her. Once she laid her head on his chest, his arms circled around her, pulling her closer. She waited for him to speak, but instead, his snores grew louder. Evelyn risked too much by lying in his arms. If he awoke, it would appear that she had forgiven him.

She tried to slip away, but Reese's arms locked tighter. When he remained sleeping, Evelyn relaxed and promised herself a few moments more.

"Evelyn," Reese mumbled in his sleep. Evelyn's heart clenched, hearing his yearning.

She closed her eyes, drifting to sleep with the hope that her husband wanted her filling her heart.

Chapter Fourteen

A warm cocoon cushioned Reese as he wrapped Evelyn in his arms. Utter bliss of his wife's soft body wrapped around him helped to ease a problem nagging at him.

Evelyn's soft sighs tempted him to forget his troubles… until she slipped from his arms and drifted away. Reese reached for her, but she kept avoiding his grasp. With each step he took closer to her, the heavy clouds disappeared, enveloping him into the darkness.

"Evelyn!" he called.

She glanced over her shoulder, beckoning him to follow her. However, he couldn't reach her.

When he lost sight of Evelyn and could no longer hear her, he screamed her name over and over, falling deeper and deeper into a pit of despair. He spun in circles, searching for any sign of her as the sky opened up and rained down upon him. He lifted his head as the drops soaked him, and then he heard Evelyn. She was crying her grief, her sobs floating to his ears, asking why over and over.

He had to find Evelyn.

He needed to hold her and beg for her to love him. Reese was suffocating, unable to breathe without Evelyn in his arms. He needed her.

"Evelyn!" Reese screamed, his hoarse voice grating across his ears.

Reese gasped, lurching off the bed. The bedroom door slung open, and Graham rushed inside, looking around. When he noticed Reese was still in bed, he shook his head in disgust before closing the door with a slam.

Reese winced, grabbing his head in agony, which only made Graham chuckle with amusement. However, his brother's torture wasn't through. He threw the drapes open, and sunshine scorched Reese's eyes. He lifted his arms to cover his face, but even that was painful. Reese flopped back on the bed, groaning in agony.

"A right beautiful day. Such a shame you have missed the majority of it," said Graham.

"Wha …" Reese cleared the scratchiness from his throat. "What time is it?"

Graham pulled his timepiece from his pocket, noted the time, and returned the watch. "Three o'clock in the afternoon."

Reese sighed in disgust, keeping his eyes closed. The bright light and noise kept his head pounding. He lay there wondering what the hell had happened yesterday to leave him in this state. Had he fallen ill? His body ached like the devil, and his stomach felt like revolting.

"When did you arrive?"

"Yesterday afternoon. Do you not remember?" There was something in his brother's voice he couldn't quite name.

He wracked his brain but came up with nothing. "I recall nothing since yesterday morning."

"Nothing? Not one conversation or humiliation?"

Humiliation? Who would Reese humiliate? "No, should I?"

"Humph."

Reese didn't understand what his brother was angling toward. Nor did he care. He only wished for a hot bath and something to settle his stomach. However, he wondered why Graham had returned to the city. Especially since Reese had learned the reason for his brother's departure a few weeks earlier. Another problem Reese would have to concern himself over. Why couldn't Graham stay out of trouble? What possessed Graham to involve himself with the peers he did?

"Why have you returned?"

The bed dipped as Graham sat down on the edge. "I have business to take care of and far be it from me to decline a ride to town."

"Who did you travel with?"

"Lord and Lady Sinclair."

"Did Evelyn join your traveling party?" Reese whispered.

He hoped so. It would give Reese a chance to apologize to his wife and make amends. What better location to cater to his wife's wishes than London? She could spend time with her family. Reese knew how much Evelyn missed them. He could escort her to all the finest parties and balls. It would cut into his budget, but he would spoil her with new dresses and bonnets. Perhaps even treat her to the opera or a play. Anything she wanted, as long as she forgave him for his deception. He wanted to earn her love.

No. He needed to earn her love.

"Yes, she did."

Reese released the breath he was holding in anticipation. Soon, he sprung out of bed, his illness overshadowed by the desire to hold his wife and plead for her forgiveness. He yelled for Kemp to prepare a bath and bring him something to eat. He started discarding his clothing, wondering why he still wore yesterday's attire. He never slept in his clothes.

His distraction didn't last long when he faced the mirror and took in his haggard appearance. Reese's hair stood on end, both of his eyes were a horrible shade of purple, and he was only half-dressed. His feet were bare, and the placket of his trousers and his shirt were unbuttoned.

Reese swung his gaze to his brother and met Graham's glower. "What in the hell happened to my face?"

"You do not recall a single thing from our arrival?"

Reese grimaced. "Should I?"

Graham looked at him with…was that pity in his eyes? "Oh, dear brother, you are in worst shape than I thought."

"How so?"

Graham only shook his head before settling on a chair near the window. He gazed out with his lips pinched. Graham must inform Reese how he pushed himself off the ledge, and the only way for him to climb back to victory would be to grovel at his wife's feet. He wondered how Reese would react to this bit of news.

"Well," Reese growled, losing patience.

"Well—"

"Wait," Reese interrupted. "Before you explain the state I am supposedly in, please tell me, how is Evelyn?"

Graham scowled. "There is no supposedly. You are in a disreputable state. As for how is Evelyn, that is a troublesome question to answer. On our journey, I saw a different side to Evelyn."

"How so?"

"While your wife is a charming companion to converse with, she is an utter delight when surrounded by her family. I have never seen her so carefree or silly."

Reese frowned, hardly believing it. "Evelyn, silly?"

Graham smiled, remembering the prank Evelyn and Charlotte played on him. "Yes, silly."

"All right. So Evelyn is in good spirits." Reese crossed his arms. "Do you think she will find it in her heart to forgive me for the outburst I had before I left?"

"I think she already had."

"Excellent." Reese glanced to the adjoining door. "Is she in her room?"

Graham shook his head. "No, she is not at home. Charlotte arrived a few hours ago and they are paying a visit with their family."

"Then I have time to freshen before her return."

Reese strode to the door and yelled for Kemp again, impatient that they were taking so long with his bath. Then he went to his wardrobe and threw out his attire for the day, the bruises on his face forgotten. The only thought consuming Reese was his wife. He had another chance. Only this time, he would set out not to ruin his chances at winning Evelyn's love.

"However…"

Reese turned at Graham's sound of doom. "However?"

"However, I do not think Evelyn will forgive you for the way you slandered her good name yesterday. Not only did you accuse your wife and me of an extramarital affair, though not of an affair per se, but you gave your permission to partake in one in front of the Sinclairs and the servants."

Reese dropped a handful of cravats he held in his hand at Graham's declaration. Flashes of yesterday afternoon played a scene before him. A scene where he'd degraded his wife and her character. When he closed his eyes, he only saw the pain in hers. It all came flooding back, every nasty accusation, every slap, every punch. He deserved all of it.

"No," Reese whispered.

"Yes."

"Has Evelyn left me?"

"At this time, no. However, Sinclair declared his intentions on informing the Duke of Colebourne of your deplorable treatment of his niece. If you thought to present your marriage of a loving companionship to the duke, then your time has passed. Any settlement you may have anticipated receiving, the duke will now deny."

Reese slumped in the chair next to his brother, leaning his head back. In his drunken state, he had declared his wife a strumpet, gave room for the servants to gossip about her and never earn their respect, and ruined any chance she ever had to hold her head high among the ton. Their impromptu marriage already held one strike against her. Now his talk of allowing her to spread her thighs for his brother would never grant her an invitation. No matter what power her uncle held, his slander would force Evelyn to spend her remaining life in the country. Exactly like his mother.

While their circumstances were different, they would hold the same isolation. Even though, at one time, that had been his intention for Evelyn after she deceived him and caused him to lose the investment to further his breeding program. Now, because of his drunkenness, his family would remain destitute. There would be no settlement from the Duke of Colebourne. He would have to sell his livestock to keep the family afloat.

The door opened wider, and the servants carried in hot water for his bath. His valet hustled to the wardrobe to straighten the mess Reese had made. A maid carried in a platter of sandwiches and tea. Rogers followed the maid with a smaller tray holding a bottle of whiskey and two tumblers.

"Leave this room now!" Reese ordered the servants.

Graham rose. "Thank you. I apologize for my brother. I am afraid he is still a bit indisposed."

However, before each servant left, they regarded him with distaste. They no longer held a look of respect in their eyes.

"Our poor mistress." Reese heard the maid mutter under her breath when she walked by.

He stared after them, his fury building. How dare these lowly beings treat him with disrespect. He gave them employment, paid their wages, and offered them free room and board. It was on the tip of his tongue to fire the lot of them and start from scratch again. Then it dawned on him. They paid their loyalty to Evelyn now, not him.

Graham stared at Reese with clear disgust. "Yes. Quite an amazing staff Rogers has hired. Each one of them holds sympathy for Evelyn. All throughout the day I have listened to their pledges and answered their questions concerning your behavior. Even though I wished to portray you as the arse you are, I declined. Instead, I blamed your excessive amount of drinking you partook in as the reason for your insanity. I reassured them it was not normal behavior and that you only drank because of the sincere depth of feelings you held for your wife and because you missed her tremendously after being apart from her for so long. It was the first time you spent apart since you wed and you felt like you were going mad with longing, considering Evelyn was the other half of your soul."

Was this what Reese had been reduced to?

Graham rolled his eyes. "It seemed to fool them for the time being. How long before they know the truth, I cannot tell. That, my brother, is in your hands." He stood. "Now if you will excuse me, I need to visit the club before my dinner plans."

"Evelyn and I can have time alone this evening."

"I am afraid not. The Duke of Colebourne has issued me an invitation to dine with his family this evening. I am eager to meet the rest of Evelyn's family. If they are half as delightful as her, it shall be a grand evening."

"Excellent, I shall meet you at the club and we can take my carriage to dinner." Reese started undressing.

Graham winced. "Colebourne did not extend the invitation toward you."

"What?" Reese growled.

"The invitation specifically excluded your presence. The duke sent another letter along, explaining that if you were to show your face, you would be escorted off the premises."

"That is outlandish."

Graham crossed his arms. "Is it, Reese? Are you even aware of how you have torn Evelyn's reputation to shreds? It is by her good grace and actions that your servants have not spread yesterday's ordeal around to the other households. So far, no rumors are spreading. But for how long? All it will take is for any servant in this house to have a slip of the tongue and your wife will be a pariah. While you strut around London, unblemished. I can hear the whispers now. Can you?"

Reese closed his eyes in defeat. "Yes."

"Do you promise to stay away?"

"Will you bring Evelyn home after dinner?" Reese pleaded.

"If she wishes to return. If not, then you must respect her wishes. She deserves so much more than what you have offered her. Evelyn does not deserve the treatment you have displayed, nor has she ever."

Reese could only nod in agreement. His throat grew thick with regret. The words he wanted to utter stuck, refusing to come out. Everything his brother spoke was God's honest truth. He was a selfish bastard, using Evelyn like he had. All for what, revenge? He couldn't even remember any more. Graham spoke with honesty on his explanation to the servants. It was the exact reason he drank himself to oblivion. He had finally realized the depth of his love for Evelyn, and it scared him. Now Reese feared he had ruined any chance to live happily ever after with her. All because of jealousy.

"I shall see you on my return."

After Graham left, Reese eased his aching muscles into the hot water. Steam billowed around him. He tipped his head over the rim of the tub, resting his arms on the edge. He didn't know how long he lay there for. The water had long grown cold. The chill was nothing compared to the ice running through his veins. Each word he threw at Evelyn replayed over and over, stealing the warmth from his body.

As he felt remorse for his actions, he also grew more confident about how he could win Evelyn back. Ideas kept forming one after another. His newfound determination prompted him into action.

He finished bathing and dried off. Reese didn't call for Kemp to dress him. He dressed in a leisurely fashion since he would remain at home this evening, making plans to win Evelyn's heart. He slipped on trousers, leaving his feet bare, and pulled on a white chambray shirt over his head. It was one he wore when working with the horses. He saw no need to be uncomfortable in his own home. It wasn't like there would be any visitors this evening. Also, he planned to make himself scarce if Graham persuaded Evelyn to return home. Reese owed her an apology, but he didn't quite know how to humble himself at her feet.

Chapter Fifteen

Reese padded over to the adjoining door, peeled it open, and searched the bedroom to make sure Evelyn hadn't returned. When he saw the bedroom empty, he opened the door wider and strode around the room. He inhaled the fragrance of Evelyn that perfumed the air.

He walked to the vanity and lifted a bottle of perfume to smell the sweet scent. His fingers ran over the hairbrush next to the variety of ribbons and hair bobs that lay in a neat line. He opened the lid to a small trinket and noticed it full of buttons. Reese trailed his fingers over the decorations and realized they were the buttons from her wedding nightgown that he had ripped from her body. Their wedding night was ingrained in his memory as the most pleasurable of encounters he had shared with Evelyn. He placed the trinket back on the vanity.

His steps took him to the divan where a book lay open. Reese sat down and started reading the page she had left off on. It was a book of poems. Not just any poems, but love poems. The opened page had a heart-wrenching piece about a love unrequited. The poet poured their emotions into words of a love freely given but never returned. Heartache leapt from the pages, causing Reese's guilt to notch another ring higher. His eyes devoured the poem.

When he finished, he traced his fingers over the words as if he were trying to soothe their bruised edges. Evelyn had creased the top of the page to find it again. He knew she resonated with the passage. Every word written was the actions of a selfish bastard set on revenge to destroy the victim. The words described him. Reese wondered how to fix the mess he had created.

He kicked his legs up and settled amongst the cushions. His head rested on the nest of pillows and he turned on his side, flipping the pages of the book. Evelyn had dog-eared other pages. He read every poem that had touched her heart. Not every sonnet was of a tragic love never returned. No, there were others filled with love and hope. Evelyn even made notations on the pages, remarking on passages that held an impact on her.

A few hours later, Reese had more insight into how he could woo his wife. He would need to proceed with caution and treat her like the treasure she was.

Reese reached the end of the book and paused. There were a few pages filled with Evelyn's hand. She'd dated the pages, starting with last December. As he started reading, Reese realized that Evelyn had used the back of the book as a journal, detailing her most intimate thoughts. He closed the book. He didn't dare read her private memories. No. Reese debated with himself to drop the book and leave Evelyn's room. He had taken so much away from her already. He had no business stealing what was only for Evelyn to cherish.

However, the weak side of him held all the strength. He made himself a promise. He would only read the passages to help him better understand how to proceed with his wife. And for no other reason. He wouldn't use Evelyn's words to help seduce her. No, that would be too devious.

Reese opened the book to the back and devoured every word Evelyn had written. His guilty conscience kept tugging at him to cease, but her words held him entranced to continue.

December 27th, 1821 ~ *Before bed*

The festivities continue and the air is lively. My family embraces the holiday season with gusto, each day more joyous than the last. We have a guest staying with us this year. He arrived the day after Christmas. Lucas's friend from school, Lord Reese Worthington. I heard Lucas explain to Uncle Theo that Worthington needed a place to stay while he came to terms with his new standings. His father recently passed, and Worthington is now an earl. During dinner, Worthington kept drawing my eye. I felt a connection with him deep in my soul. The pain in his eyes reflected my own. I wish I could help ease whatever troubles him.

However, it would appear Charlie enlightened his heart. Their conversation at dinner made his eyes shine. He laughed at Charlie's quirky sense of humor, and I watched him touch her hand. Not a friendly touch, but a stroke of seduction. I know I read too many romantic novels, but I saw the seductive caress of his finger slowly sliding on the edge of Charlie's hand to the tip of her finger.

Of course, Charlie was oblivious to Worthington's attention. Charlie kept rattling on about her horse, Sapphire. Which is probably why Charlie gained Worthington's notice. He has his own breeding program and loves horses as much as Charlie, if not more.

After dinner, the atmosphere in the drawing room continued in the same manner. Worthington never strayed far from Charlie's side. When we sang carols, he coaxed Charlie into singing a duet with him. Then, before we retired for the evening, he convinced Charlie to join Lucas and him on an early morning ride. Charlie needed no encouragement. Only Charlie grew frustrated when Sinclair said he would meet them too. Sinclair joined our family for dinner, like he does every week.

I should not laugh, but it was a comical affair to watch. Charlie kept growing more agitated with Sinclair. I wonder when Charlie and Sinclair will realize the attraction that sizzles between them. Oh, how I ache to experience that emotion with another. Would it singe immediately, or would it slowly burn into an inferno of passion out of control?

I think I will go to the library to find a book to read to take my mind off my twisted emotions. I feel off-center as if the universe is sending me toward a direction that I am unsure where to follow. A book will help to settle me, it always does.

~~~

December 27th, 1821 ~ *After a visit to the library*

Oh, my! Oh, my! If I thought I was unsettled before, I am a wreck now. I cannot believe I allowed myself to act so wantonly. But I could not help myself. His teasing nature, his gentle caress ... Oh, my! Not to mention the lightening effect of his lips as they pressed to mine. Not pressed. No, too tame of a word. Devoured. Yes, devoured is the correct term.

I should have left immediately. But when he drew me into his arms and settled me onto his lap, wrapping his arms around me in a tingling embrace, I became lost. Lost in love. Is it foolish to profess my love for him so soon? Love at first sight only exists in silly novels. It is not for real. However, I now know that to be false. I love Reese Worthington with all my heart. As his kisses continued, I only fell harder. He drew my sweetness inside of him, his gentle caresses awakened me from the fog I had existed in for so many years. His embrace wrapped me in a cocoon of security. I had finally found my home.

....

Or so I thought.

~~~~~

Reese grew confused. She thought? What did that mean? His mind drifted back to that evening, recalling each of her memories with his own. He had been reading, trying to forget his troubles, when an angel appeared in the doorway dressed in a white nightgown with her hair tumbling around her shoulders in disarray. When she noticed him, she'd paused in her tracks, her mouth opening in surprise. A mouth that tugged at his insides. His throat had dried, and he sat spellbound at the beauty before him. Never had he experienced an attraction so strong. He wondered why he hadn't felt it during dinner and afterwards singing with her. However, he didn't stop to ponder why.

He'd strode to her side before she left and teased her about a kiss she had to grant him for interrupting him. Her blush grew, and she tried to back away. But Reese would have none of that. He had to kiss her. No, he needed a kiss like an addict needed a drug. Her petal-soft lips beckoned him closer. When she tipped her head up to meet his tease, he didn't hesitate to take what she so freely offered. It was at that moment Reese lost himself. Lost to every emotion he thought he possessed. Her kiss knocked him senseless. He wanted more. No. Reese craved more. Her whispered sighs echoed in his soul. How would she sound when she moaned? Or when she screamed?

Reese discovered the husky moans that whispered past her lips. They were music to his ears. He had swept her on his lap, plying her with more kisses and gentle caresses. How he craved more, but if he continued, he knew he would take her innocence. As tempting of a package she was, he wasn't able to offer for her hand. The last thing he needed was a bride.

So, Reese pushed his urges down and advised her to return to her bedroom before he ruined both of their lives. To remove himself from any further temptations, he left the next morning before anyone had risen. He would miss their ride in the morning, but he would never forget the taste of her lips, her intoxicating scent, or the softness of her touch against him.

Reese had left for London to appease his appetite with one of his mistresses. But when he paid them a visit, an innocent angel consumed his thoughts. He left Angelica and Barbara in a tiff at his inadequate attention, promising he would make it worth their while when he returned. However, he never did. Reese didn't want to sully his memories of an innocent temptress with tawdry affairs. So, he returned home to his estate and worked to put his affairs in order. Perhaps if he became solvent, the Duke of Colebourne would grant him permission to court his ward. If not, then Reese planned to make her his any way he could.

Reese glanced back at the page, needing to appease his curiosity at why Evelyn had changed her mind about their tryst.

~~~~~

.... It was a magical moment when my heart broke free and embraced the spark of life. But the name he whispered was not my own. My fragile heart fell, flipping over and over and shattering into a million pieces. My Prince Charming, who awakened me with his kiss, did not kiss me, Evelyn Holbrooke. No, he kissed Charlotte Holbrooke, my sister. My twin. The word devastation now fills my soul.

~~~~~

"Damn," Reese growled.

He tore his hand through his hair in frustration. Evelyn's heartbreak leapt from the pages, tearing a rip in his heart. From their earliest connection, he had caused her pain and continued to do so today.

~~~~~

January 20th, 1822

I need to forget him, but I cannot. Every night when I close my eyes and drift to sleep, he comes to me in my dreams, coaxing away more kisses. I think I could handle these thoughts if they were only in my dreams. But they happen throughout the day at the most inappropriate times. At breakfast, at lunch, at dinner. How am I am supposed to carry a conversation when I forget what I am talking about?

Grhh.

~~~

February 25th, 1822

Lord Reese Worthington

Lady Evelyn Worthington

Countess Evelyn Worthington

Lord and Lady Worthington

~~~~~

Reese's smile grew wide at Evelyn's wishes.

~~~~

March 15th, 1822

Uncle Theo surprised the family at dinner with an announcement. He decided to give all of us girls a London season. I tried to hold back my excitement at this news, but it proved to be too difficult. With a season, it will give me a chance to see Lord Worthington. When we arrive in town, we will surely receive invitations to the same balls and entertainments. It will be my chance to charm him. I know I will have to break free from my shyness, but for him I will.

Not everyone holds the same excitement, though. Abigail snuck away at the first opportunity. I can understand why, but still it bothered me. However, Uncle Theo made it very clear that Abigail is to join us in the festivities. In the morning, I shall talk with her to help ease her worries.

Charlie, on the other hand, is furious with Uncle Theo's plans. She sees no reason for a season. Charlie does not want a husband. She is perfectly content with the horses. Nor does she need a season, in my opinion. Once Jasper Sinclair realizes the depths of his emotions for Charlie, my sister will not have to endure the upcoming season.

Jacqueline has kept her joy at a minimum. I think she will enjoy London, but I worry that she is very set in her ways and the man that captures her heart will have to be a resourceful gentleman to keep Jacqueline on her toes. However, Gemma shares my enthusiasm for our adventure. We poured over the fashion plates all evening and made plans on the sights we want to visit upon our arrival. I cannot wait.

~~~

April 1st, 1822

I might not have to wait for the London season after all. Uncle Theo has arranged a house party in our honor. He has invited many eligible bachelors as his guests, plus a few debutantes he thinks we will form friendships with. I hope Lord Worthington is one of the guests. I cannot wait.

Aunt Susanna is coming to help us learn how to organize such an event. I have missed her tremendously. She is so comforting. How I wish I could confide in her and ask for advice. But I cannot. I must keep my secret, for I do not wish for Uncle Theo to become involved. I love him dearly, but he can be a bit high-handed in granting each of us our greatest wishes. I do not want Lord Worthington to feel forced to offer for my hand. No. I wish for him to realize that he cannot live without me, and he will do anything to make me his. Is this a foolish wish?

~~~

April 10th, 1822

He is coming. Lord Worthington will be a guest at the house party. I cannot contain the thrill coursing through my veins. Gemma pilfered the guest list, made a copy, and returned it before Uncle Theo realized it was missing. The list contained gentlemen's names with the date of the house party written on top. Next to each gentleman's name was a notation written in code. I am sure each code holds a meaning. But I do not care. The only thing I care about is that he will arrive in five days and stay for an entire week. Can I make him fall in love with me in such a short time?

~~~

April 15th, 1822

He has arrived. It has been over four months since I saw him last. The old saying about time making the heart grow fonder pales compared to the emotions rushing through me. He has only grown more handsome and charming. However, he still has a look of sadness in his gaze. Not only sadness, but also a hint of desperation. I want to soothe them away and replace them with happiness. I had hoped to have a chance after dinner to speak with him, but Lord Sinclair asked me to walk with him instead. I wanted to refuse, but knew I could not.

After we returned from our walk, Worthington was no longer in the drawing room. Neither was Charlie. I wondered if Lord Worthington coaxed Charlie away. But when I returned to our bedroom, Charlie was fast asleep. I cannot even describe the sense of relief I felt at seeing her lying in her bed, snoring away, oblivious to my state of mind. My greatest fear is that Charlie finds Worthington a worthy fellow. Her frustration with Sinclair has been more than obvious. If Worthington paid Charlie any attention, will my sister turn her regards to him? They share the same interests. They both love the outdoors and horseflesh. I pray not. Tomorrow, I promise myself I will attempt to draw his notice.

~~~

April 16th, 1822

I cannot stop my shaking. I want to burst into a song about my joyous emotions. This day could not have passed by more fabulous. I hope it does so again tomorrow.

After I confided in Charlie about my feelings for Worthington, we concocted a plan for him to take notice. Now that I sit and write this, the full justification of our actions settles in my gut. The deception gnaws at my conscience, begging for me to be honest. But I cannot. I worry Worthington will find me not to his liking.

Aunt Susanna paired Charlie with Worthington for the afternoon entertainment of pall-mall, but we switched places. When we were younger, we performed this act many times, fooling our loved ones. We had not done so in years. However, the temptation was too strong. We excused ourselves and switched clothing. Worthington held no clue it was I who was his partner for the afternoon.

Throughout the game, he charmed me with his charismatic humor, teased me with his flirtation, and placed gentle touches when no one watched. If I did not love him before, I fear I fell harder today. My memories keep replaying every memory of our time together. I cannot even sleep this night. I am excited for tomorrow when I can be in his company once again. Tomorrow, please hurry.

~~~

April 19th, 1822

I feel my dreams slipping slowly away with each passing day. I am no closer to having Worthington fall in love with me than the day before. When he stole me away to steal kisses, I thought I had made progress. But when we are in the presence of others, Worthington ignores me. He even appears irritated with my company. His persistence to have Charlie notice him hurts deeply. I know in my heart that Charlie holds no feelings for Worthington, but it still does not stop the jealousy clawing away at my shredded emotions. I thought I had finally gotten through to him when I touched his hand as we waited for Aunt Susanna to announce the afternoon festivities. The rain kept us inside the past two days and the gentlemen grew restless. I suffer from the same inflection. After I touched him, Worthington stopped focusing on Charlie and directed his attention toward me. I broke free from my shyness and talked with him. I talked to him as Evelyn, not under the cover of Charlie. And I saw the interest sparkle in his eyes, if only for a moment. It was there. I did not imagine it.

However, after Aunt Susanna paired us for the scavenger hunt, I lost his attention. He became obsessed with learning everything about Charlie and kept dragging me along, trying to find where Charlie and Sinclair had disappeared to. When he could not find them, he grew more agitated. When Charlie and Sinclair returned to the drawing room, it was more than apparent how they spent the past two hours. While I am more than happy for my sister, I cannot stop the despair settling in my heart.

~~~

April 20th, 1822

I confessed my love for Worthington to Jacqueline, Gemma, and Abigail today. Their support humbled me. I always knew I held their love, but their advice and guidance helped to ease my heartache. The ball is in two days. It will be my last attempt to capture Worthington's heart.

Charlie and I switched places again this evening, and I enjoyed myself immensely with Worthington throughout dinner. However, I saw the deceit for what it represented. I also realized that I deserve more. I deserve to have

Worthington's unwavering attention meant for me alone, not for who he thinks I am. When I dress for the ball's festivities, I will do so for me. I may not have won the love of the man I adore, but I have emerged from the shell I have hidden myself in since my parent's death. When they died, a part of me died with them. I have lived in fear of living. However, the most important lesson I have learned this week is how to love myself. When Worthington leaves, he will take away a part of my heart he does not even realize he holds, and I will bear a most wrenching heartache. But I will survive.

After all, I am a Holbrooke.

Under Evelyn's declaration, she drew two hearts. One whole, the other broken. She wrote under them:

> *Which heart will win?*

~~~

April 21st, 1822

I have lost something I never held.

~~~~~

Reese paused again in his reading, trying to remember that week. He racked his memories for any sign of why Evelyn felt like she had lost. He knew Evelyn referred to him. What happened?

~~~~~

April 22nd, 1822 ~ *During the ball*

I cannot stop the tears. I thought I could handle this, but I cannot. He still sees me as nothing more than a nuisance or an invisible being. Why did I imagine I could capture his attention? He has asked Charlie for the dinner dance, in which he will escort her to dinner. I know Charlie only told him yes so he would leave her alone. Charlie fixated her attention on her search for Sinclair. Once Sinclair arrived, Charlie hurried to his side and left me all alone on the edge of the dance floor. My gaze searched for Worthington to find him laughing alongside Lucas. I saw the triumph in his eyes. He thought he won Charlie.

~~~

Charlie just left with Lucas. Sapphire has gone into labor. I know what I am about to do is wrong. However, I am powerless to stop myself from my last attempt to win Reese. My love. As I stood before the mirror, I brushed out my hair into billowing waves around my shoulders and smoothed the material of Charlie's dress over my hips. I promise this will be the last time.

~~~

April 23rd, 1822

Every emotion a person could experience, I have gone through on this day. In the earliest of the morning hours, I floated on clouds of ecstasy, then fell into a crushing heap of defeat. I have made my bed, and now I must lie in it. The depth of my deception is now known. If I imagined once that when Reese learned the truth he will love me, I now know I played myself false. All Reese Worthington feels for me is disgust, anger, and loathing. And I deserve these emotions. I caused them. But do I regret them? No. Because if I had never deceived him, I would never have experienced what I did. I only hope that one day I can seek his forgiveness. I promise from this day forth, I will never lie to him again. He may only see me as the dull sister, but I pledge before our life together is over, he will experience the passion I am capable of.

~~~

April 25th, 1822

Today I married Lord Reese Worthington. It included a hurried carriage ride to Gretna Green and vows performed by a blacksmith. Instead of resting for the day, we made the return journey toward his home, which will now be my home. A home I know Reese will abandon me to. I only hope I can make him see me in a better light once we settle into our marriage. Our carriage ride has proved to be very enlightening. I will not let him cower me with his arrogance.

Worthington changed his mind and stopped at an inn. Now I wait for him to join me for a meal.

I hope for more.

Am I a fool in all this madness?

~~~~~~

No, Evelyn, 'tis he who was the fool. A fool who had the most amazing woman in the world at his feet and destroyed her with his foolish rantings. Reese didn't need to read anymore to understand the depth of Evelyn's emotions, nor did he want to read in fear that she no longer held love for him.

He rose and laid the book as he had found it. He wanted to remain in the room and wait for Evelyn to return, but he didn't wish to scare her away. On his way out, Reese slipped the buttons into his pocket.

Reese stared out the window in his own bedroom. He didn't realize when the sky had darkened and how late it had grown. He only knew that his wife and brother hadn't returned yet. Reese grew impatient. However, he refused to leave his position. He waited with bated breath for the carriage to arrive.

When Rogers arrived with dinner, Reese refused to eat, his stomach unsettled over wondering if he'd lost Evelyn's love. When the house grew quiet and one hour after another passed by, Reese admitted defeat.

He stretched his weary body on the soft mattress and closed his eyes. It was then that a memory flashed before him. Evelyn making him more comfortable. Evelyn's gentle caresses over his bruises. Evelyn snuggling into him, warming him. His arms wrapping around and holding her as close as he could. He remembered sighing her name.

Reese thought it had all been a dream. However, it had been real. Evelyn was real. It gave him hope that Evelyn still loved him.

Chapter Sixteen

Reese waited at the table for Evelyn to come downstairs for breakfast. He had risen early, so as not to miss her. He'd asked the cook to make Evelyn's favorite breakfast—jam-filled pastries and tea—then he walked through the garden and cut a rose to lie next to her plate. He told Rogers to deliver the mail and newspapers to his study. He would read them later.

For now, he wished to make himself available to Evelyn. Reese sat waiting patiently. However, she never came belowstairs. He didn't want to inquire to the servants of her whereabouts. From their coldness, they would do him no favors. The only reason the cook agreed was because Reese told her of Evelyn's favorite foods.

When he heard footsteps coming along the hallway, Reese rose from his chair to welcome Evelyn. His hope deflated when Graham strolled into the room. Where could she be?

Graham glanced about the dining room for the breakfast buffet, but nothing was prepared. Then he noticed the table's leaves reduced to one and sat for an intimate breakfast for two. He raised his brows at Reese. Then his eyes focused on the pastries and he reached for one.

"No," Reese growled.

Graham paused with his hand in mid-air. "Why not?"

"Those are for Evelyn."

Graham sighed. "Fine."

He pulled out the chair to sit down, but Reese voiced his displeasure and stopped him before he could. "You need to visit your club for breakfast. That seat is for when Evelyn arrives."

However, Graham ignored Reese and sat. He noticed the romantic gesture near the plate and picked up the rose. He inhaled the perfume scent and laid it across the plate. "Evelyn chose not to return home last night. She decided to visit with her family more."

Reese's hope slowly seeped away. He slumped into his chair, dejected. All his efforts to make breakfast pleasurable and apologize were for naught. Evelyn wasn't even at home. Would she even return?

Reese cleared his throat. "Did her family learn of ..." He couldn't finish asking if everyone knew of his misdeeds.

"Yes. Sinclair informed Colebourne and Gray. Charlie confided to the other ladies in the family if their cold regard toward me were anything to go by during dinner."

"Guilty by association?" Reese's words dripped with sarcasm.

"At first. However, halfway through the dinner, Evelyn scolded her family for their rudeness. She explained to them how I have offered her support since the first day we met. Then their manner warmed toward me. I must say I had a most enjoyable evening."

"Humph."

"Her cousin Gemma is a treasure." Graham grabbed a pastry.

Reese held up his hand. "Stop."

"What?"

"You will stay away from Gemma Holbrooke. You do not want to involve yourself with the Duke of Colebourne's machinations."

"Perhaps I do." Graham took a bite of the pastry.

"Really?" Reese arched an eyebrow in disbelief.

"No." Graham sighed. "But she is a delightful temptation."

"She is not for you. It does not matter anyway. The duke has already chosen a gentleman for Gemma."

"Who?"

Reese arched a brow. "Does it matter?"

Graham shrugged, pretending indifference.

Reese rose. "I do not know, except every gentleman invited to his house party had their purpose. And that was to fall in love with one of his wards. Since Colebourne did not invite you, he will not welcome your attentions toward Lady Gemma. It would be best if you stayed clear, and absolutely no flirting. My own troubles with that family are insurmountable. I do not wish to take on yours, too."

"Yes, I suppose." Graham reached inside his suit coat and pulled out a missive. "Before I forget, Colebourne has summoned you to his lair."

Reese opened the letter. Colebourne demanded his presence. He didn't state a time, so that meant Reese was already late by the duke's standards. He stalked out of the room. Reese only hoped he could redeem himself in the duke's eyes. Since he knew the duke would summon him, Reese had already prepared a speech. After he met with Colebourne, he would find his wife and humble himself before her.

"Reese?"

Reese paused, turning slightly.

"I am sorry Evelyn did not see your effort. Her heartstrings would have tugged in response. Do not despair, I believe you still hold a chance."

Reese nodded. He met Rogers in the hallway and ordered the carriage. He hurried to his study to write a note to Evelyn in case she refused to see him. His hand scrawled the romantic lines from a poem she'd marked in her book. With a smile, Reese strolled with a new sense of confidence he'd lost for a moment when he learned Evelyn hadn't returned home.

~~~~~

Evelyn smiled wistfully at Gemma. Her cousin was sighing over Graham's charming attributes. Her cousin was smitten, but Evelyn didn't think Graham was the gentleman for Gemma. Evelyn loved him like a brother, but he wasn't ready to commit. No more than his brother, obviously. Perhaps they both took after their father more than they realized. Evelyn needed to keep a watch on her cousin and steer her in a different direction if the flirtation between the two went too far.

Evelyn had missed these early morning breakfasts with her sisters, cousin, and friend. Abigail wasn't related by blood, but they considered her their sister. When a boating accident killed their parents, leaving them orphans, Uncle Theo had taken them all under his wing and loved them like they were his own. Abigail's mother had been Gemma's mother's maid. When she perished, Uncle Theo never thought twice and brought Abigail to live with them, too.

"Will you be sending for your luggage?" asked Jacqueline.

Evelyn raised her head, her musings clearing away. For a minute, while thinking of Graham and Gemma, she had fallen into her usual trap of obsessing over Reese. She wondered what it would feel like to have a gentleman flirt with her out of interest for her alone and not as an attempt to gain a horse. A gentleman who knew exactly who she was.

However, Evelyn didn't want any gentleman. She only wanted Reese.

Evelyn wandered toward the window. "No."

"No?" every lady asked at once.

"No. I shall return after I have a private word with Uncle Theo."

"Have you grown mad?" Charlie rose.

Evelyn understood Charlie's dismay, for she had witnessed Reese's cruelty, not once but twice. Or did yesterday afternoon count as the third incident? Either way, it didn't matter. Evelyn planned to return to Reese on her terms. She knew Uncle Theo would provide support. The ending was the same. She loved Reese. He had only lashed out on their arrival from pain. His other outbursts had resulted from her deceit. A man's pride was his downfall. Evelyn wasn't innocent in this affair. If it weren't for her deception, her husband would trust her. However, their marriage hadn't started off on the right foot. It had been a disaster since she admitted to her dishonesty.

"Duncan said our deceit would not end well," Charlie plopped back down.

Evelyn turned around. "He did? How did he find out?"

"I confided in him and he told me we needed to be honest. He warned that the consequences of our actions would not be pleasant. That when you fooled a gentleman, you damaged his pride. I suppose Worthington's ego did not take lightly to our game."

"Not his ego, Charlie. But his feelings. You might consider Worthington an arrogant arse, but he is my arrogant arse. All he had was his pride, and we trampled it to shreds with our selfish acts. I am as much to blame for the condition of our marriage as Worthington."

"Jacqueline, tell her it is not safe for her to return to Worthington," Charlie begged their older sister.

Jacqueline directed a pensive stare at Evelyn. "Is Worthington violent?"

"No," answered Evelyn.

"He may not be with his fists, but his words say otherwise," argued Charlie.

"Is your life at risk?" asked Gemma.

Evelyn shook her head. "No."

"Does he flaunt his mistresses in your face?" asked Abigail.

"No." Evelyn sat back down.

"Is his family kind to you?" asked Jacqueline.

"Yes." Evelyn smiled. "They welcomed me as one of their own."

Charlie rose again and swept her hand out. "Tell them how furious he was when he discovered the paperwork for Cobalt was only in your name."

"Why did you do that?" Abigail asked Charlie.

"Because." Charlie would offer no other explanation.

"So, let me get this straight. You taunted Cobalt at Worthington, then pulled the foal away, knowing full well how important the horse would be for his circumstances. You provoked him into reacting angrily," Jacqueline accused. "Did you not stop to think how he would react? How it would reflect on Evelyn."

Charlie sat silently, taking in Jacqueline's viewpoint. She folded her arms across her chest and tapped her foot impatiently on the floor. Everyone focused on her, waiting for a reply. She glanced at Evelyn and realized she was partly to blame for Worthington's cruelty, just as she had when he discovered the truth to their deception. She tried to imagine how Jasper would have acted if she deceived him in the same form. Would he have acted the same?

Charlie wanted to believe he wouldn't have been so cruel. But then she remembered how he'd reacted with jealousy when he thought she loved another. Had she misjudged Worthington and his depth of emotions for her sister? Now that she thought about it, when they dropped off Evelyn, Charlie had witnessed a jealous man. And she knew firsthand how one could misjudge a situation and the reaction of a jealous man. Not themselves. When Charlie slapped Worthington, he never flinched. He took his punishment because he realized the errors of his way. She saw the regret in his eyes and misjudged it for something altogether different.

Charlie raised her eyes, her own regret stirring. "Our visit triggered a reminder of our trap, and the gift fueled his fury."

Evelyn nodded. Charlie moved to Evelyn and sank to her knees. She laid her head on Evelyn's lap and apologized over and over for Evelyn's heartache. Evelyn assured Charlie she held no anger toward her.

After a while, Charlie leapt to her feet and started pacing back and forth. "We must think of a plan …"

Evelyn smiled. "No."

"No?" asked everyone again.

"No. We have no need to. My husband shall pay court very soon." Evelyn winked.

"How do you hold such confidence?" asked Gemma.

"When I spoke to Graham before he left, he informed me of Reese's condition and his deep regret. At this moment, my husband will have realized I never returned home last night. His reaction remains a mystery. I hope he misses me as much as I do him. I do not wish to make him suffer. We have each suffered enough and not held trust in one another to last a lifetime. The wishes I hold in my heart, I only want Reese to fulfill. No other."

"How may we help?" asked Charlie.

"By not doing a single thing. Life will steer the course of our reunion. If fate wishes, then our marriage will find peace. If not, then I shall have to reconsider my options. For now, I must strive to prove my love to Reese."

Chapter Seventeen

Colebourne's butler left Worthington waiting in the foyer like a commoner, not a respected peer. But then again, with his behavior of late, he deserved the treatment. However, he didn't mind. It gave him a chance to find Evelyn. He searched up and down the hallway for any sign of her. He ventured near the parlor and glanced inside, only to find the room empty.

When Worthington heard a throat clear behind him, he stiffened, then turned, feigning an arrogance that he had a right to wander through Colebourne's home.

"The duke will see you now." The butler turned, expecting Worthington to follow him.

Worthington followed the butler to the duke's study. When he entered, he noticed the duke wasn't alone. Sinclair and Gray each stood on opposite sides of the desk, presenting a united front. The duke sat regally at his desk with a scowl, demanding Worthington's undivided attention.

Worthington walked forward and stood behind a chair. He knew not to offend the duke by taking a seat without an offer made. And by the surrounding atmosphere of hostility, they would make no offer. At one time, Gray and Worthington had been the best of mates. He would never have fallen for Evelyn if not for Gray's invitation last winter. By Gray's glare, he had revoked his offer of friendship.

"Please take a seat, Worthington," the duke offered, surprising Reese.

"I prefer to stand."

Gray looked to Sinclair and nodded toward Worthington. "By your hands?" he asked, impressed with Worthington's two bruised eyes.

Sinclair raised his hand and closed it, bending his knuckles. He looked at his nails. "As if I would tarnish my hands with him." He smirked.

Worthington stayed calm. He needed to prove to Colebourne that he held control over his temper. Sinclair and Gray were only baiting him for a rise, one in which he wouldn't react to. He would endure their twisted humor for Evelyn.

Colebourne pointed to the door. "Both of you leave now!"

"But, Father…" Gray protested.

Colebourne held up his hand and interrupted his son. "No. You had your chance to defend Evelyn's honor at the house party and you did not. Instead you preoccupied yourself with another young miss. In doing so, you neglected to protect your cousin."

Worthington held a clue who the young miss might be, who wasn't Gray's intended. He never saw Gray anywhere near his betrothed, Selina Pemberton, once throughout the house party. Instead, Gray had followed Abigail Cason around like a wounded pup. Worthington wondered when Colebourne would force Gray to wed Lady Selina. Lady Selina's father had secured a promise years ago. Gray had confided in Worthington his dislike for the miss. But like all families in powerful positions, Gray didn't have the ability to choose his own bride. Colebourne had devised their union before Gray was even out of leading strings.

Once they were alone, the duke extended his hand, indicating for Worthington to sit. Reese took a seat and waited for the duke to address him.

"Would you like to present your case?"

"No. Whatever you have heard, 'tis the truth. I shamefully admit to my mistreatment of Evelyn."

Colebourne peered at Worthington shrewdly. He hadn't expected the earl to admit to his faults so easily. Even though he hadn't seen his niece's tears, he saw the heartache in her eyes. His own guilt settled heavily in the air. He wasn't an innocent bystander in this disaster of a marriage. Perhaps Lucas was correct, and he was a bit mad. He'd thought Worthington was the man for Evelyn, but now he sat conflicted with his misjudgment.

However, the more he observed Worthington, the more a kernel of doubt grew. The gentleman before him appeared as miserable as his niece had last night during dinner. Did Worthington regret his cruel actions? Could he hope the earl had fallen as hard for Evelyn as she had for him? There was only one way to discover how Worthington felt.

The duke pulled out the settlement he drew up when Evelyn's letters portrayed marital bliss. He thought Worthington had set his pride to the side and realized the gem Evelyn was. However, when Sinclair presented him with the facts of Worthington's revenge, he had been on the verge of tearing the document to shreds. Instead, he would use it to judge Worthington's true nature.

He extended the offer toward Worthington. Worthington perused it, a wrinkle appearing on his forehead, followed by a frown. Colebourne had been more than generous with him, if one considered the circumstances of the rushed marriage.

Colebourne had no intention of making Evelyn suffer because she had fallen in love with the wrong gentleman, even though Worthington had been Colebourne's choice for Evelyn when he learned of Worthington's seduction last winter. As furious as Colebourne was with Worthington, he also felt gratitude toward the man for coaxing Evelyn out of her shell to experience the joy of life again.

Worthington read over the document. The duke was presenting him the marriage settlement with the changes Worthington had requested a few weeks ago. Colebourne had been more than generous with his offer. It was more than Reese expected, considering how he had ruined Evelyn with his seduction. The amount would bring him flush and allow his family a comfortable lifestyle while he rebuilt their fortune.

However, he had to refuse it.

He considered how this would affect his family. Eden and Noel would have to postpone their debuts another year. He would have to lower Graham's allowance. Worthington would have to tighten the purse strings on any purchases his mother or Maggie might want. But they would be proud of him for rejecting it. He didn't want a fortune. He only wanted Evelyn. Without her love, Reese was only a shell of a man. He needed her to feel alive again. And he would settle for no less.

"Thank you for your generosity. I appreciate your offer considering the circumstances of my and Evelyn's union. However, I must refuse." Reese ripped the document in two and placed it on the duke's desk. "The only settlement I seek is Evelyn's love."

"A bold move." Colebourne laughed.

"'Tis no move, Your Grace. I only speak from the heart."

Colebourne studied him closely. "Yet your actions speak otherwise."

Worthington sighed with regret. "Yes, it appears they do."

"So, miraculously you love my niece?"

"I think I have all along. I had refused to admit even to myself the depth of my affection. The signs were staring me in the face the entire time.

I can see them now. However, at the time, my selfishness prevailed. My only mission was the much-needed funds for my family's survival."

Colebourne tapped his fingers on his desk, his gaze never wavering from Reese. "How has that changed? Does your family still not need funds to survive?"

"Yes, they do. However, I will secure funds from another source. When I win Evelyn's love, I want her to know that there is nothing between us but our love for one another. I need her to believe in me."

Colebourne listened to Worthington's heartfelt speech, impressed with the emotions he delivered. He would have to be a blind fool not to see how much Worthington loved Evelyn. It might have taken Worthington longer to come to the realization, but he had. However, Worthington still needed to suffer a while longer for his cruelty. Once he finished his meeting with Worthington, he would convince Evelyn to stay with him and make Worthington pay court on Evelyn like she deserved.

"I am still not convinced. That is why I plan on convincing Evelyn to remain here for the season. If you truly love her, you will court her as she deserves. Once I deem it sufficient, you may resume your marriage."

Worthington rose in agitation. "This is madness. She is already my wife and I am her husband. Because of your plotting, we never stood a chance from the very beginning. I will not agree to any more of your matchmaking attempts. I demand to see Evelyn, now."

At Worthington's outburst, Colebourne sat back in his chair and smirked. He wanted to rejoice at Worthington's demands, but didn't want to show his hand too soon. The man needed to suffer. "I refuse your request. Now, take your leave. Our appointment is over."

Worthington seethed at the duke's dismissal. He stalked to the door and threw it open. He would search this entire house for Evelyn if he had to. He refused to leave without her.

However, the duke's footmen lined the hallway with Sinclair and Gray standing at the door. Worthington knew they would use whatever force deemed necessary. He would take his leave now because he had caused Evelyn enough embarrassment. But he would return.

Before he reached the foyer, he heard someone walking down the stairs. He paused, wishing for it to be Evelyn. At first, it appeared his wish had come true, but as she drew closer, he realized it was only Charlotte. His heart rate slowed.

Charlotte paused, then continued down the stairs once she noticed Worthington. She raised her hand for him to stop. At least he thought it was for him, but he realized Sinclair had advanced on him. Worthington felt Sinclair breathing on his neck.

"Charlotte, can you please get Evelyn for me?" Worthington pleaded.

Charlotte tilted her head to the side and perused Worthington before she replied in awe, "You can tell the difference? How?"

Worthington sighed. He deserved her questioning. At one time, he had been clueless about the differences between Evelyn and Charlotte. Not any longer. "Yes."

"How?" Charlotte asked again.

"There are many ways, none that I will explain to you. I do not wish to endure your husband's wrath, or your cousin's for that matter. My brother's beating has been brutal enough." Worthington nodded his head toward Sinclair and Gray.

Charlotte inclined her head. "A fair answer."

"So will you?" Worthington asked with eagerness.

"No." Charlotte's answer was blunt and to the point.

If he climbed those steps, Worthington knew he would find Evelyn. However, he didn't know how far he would get before Sinclair and Gray stopped him. The duke had a line of footmen ready to drag him away. The only option he had was to persuade Charlotte to give his note to Evelyn. Then he would bide his time to see if she returned home. If not, then he would construct a plan to invade the duke's home.

"Will you give her this?" Worthington asked, pulling the letter out of his pocket. He handed it over to Charlotte.

To his surprise, she took it. "Yes, I will give her your letter."

"Thank you. I would like to apologize to you and Sinclair for my rude treatment while you were a guest in my home. My behavior was uncalled for, and neither of you deserved my harsh words."

Charlotte tilted her head for him to continue.

Reese swallowed and hurried ahead. "Also, I want to express my deepest regrets for not realizing the differences between Evelyn and you. My only excuse is trying to secure a financial gain, and if I am being honest, a certain lady twisted my thoughts and my heart. I could not understand how one moment she ran hot with desire and the next moment cold. In my confusion, I lost my mind. And I apologize for only pursuing you for a horse and not for the lady you were."

Charlotte's mouth hung open in surprise.

"You were correct in giving Evelyn the rights to Cobalt. I do not deserve to own such a fine creature. But I will make sure it has the best possible care for Evelyn's sake."

Charlotte studied him for several long moments before speaking. "I accept your apologies. And in return, I offer mine. I provoked you with our gift. If I am being honest, I added the stipulation because I still held onto the anger of when you so callously hurt Evelyn's feelings. I thought I was protecting my sister. But as I have come to realize my sister no longer needs my protection. She only needs my love and support. I hope we can set our differences to the side for the sake of Evelyn."

Worthington climbed another step. "Apology accepted. Does this mean I have a chance for redemption in Evelyn's eyes?"

Charlotte shrugged, her lips tilting into a smile. "Perhaps."

Worthington laughed and surprised everyone by wrapping Charlotte in a quick hug before he turned away. With a nod toward each gentleman, he strode out the door with confidence. What started out with hope had turned to despair and now returned to hope once again.

Charlotte smiled at Worthington's display of happiness. She shrugged at Jasper's and Lucas's questioning stares. With a squeak, she ran back up the stairs, eager to learn the contents of the letter. Charlotte rushed into Jacqueline's bedroom, where everyone remained drinking tea. They raised their heads at her return.

Charlotte, out of breath, waved the letter in the air. She jumped and squealed her own excitement. When she talked with Worthington, she noticed his deep remorse and the love he held for Evelyn. Her heart warmed to him and she would do anything for Evelyn to find everlasting love with Worthington. Not only for Evelyn, but for Worthington too.

"What is it?" Jacqueline inquired.

"Worthington. Visited. Letter." Charlotte gasped between each word.

"Reese is here?" Evelyn rose and hurried to the door.

"No, he has left."

"Oh."

"He left you a letter." Charlotte handed Evelyn the missive.

"Oh."

Evelyn turned and resumed her seat. She held the note in her lap. Reese arrived but didn't ask for her. He left without visiting with her. Now, his rejection lay in her hands. Were his demands and his orders to return to his estate written in his bold strokes? She traced her name on the envelope over and over. Even the way he wrote her name was a bold command. Despair clawed at her soul.

"No, no. You have it all wrong, dear," Charlotte covered Evelyn's hands with her own.

Evelyn wiped a tear from her cheek. "He did not want to pay me a visit."

"Oh, but he did. But I had to tell him no."

"Why?" asked Abigail. "You promised not to intervene anymore."

Charlotte smirked. "But I did not. You can place the blame on Jasper's and Lucas's shoulders. Or more like Uncle Theo's."

"Explain yourself," ordered Jacqueline.

"Well, as I started down the stairs, I noticed the hallway lined with footmen, and Jasper and Lucas stood at the end waiting. Soon, Worthington left Uncle Theo's office. When he saw me, he waited. You should have seen his expression. He first appeared excited, then his expression changed to disappointment. Is that not wonderful?"

"How is that wonderful?" Jacqueline narrowed her eyes.

Charlotte's smile widened. "He knew I was not Evelyn. When I questioned him on how he could tell the difference, Worthington made a most scandalous answer along the lines of not wanting to infuriate my husband further."

Evelyn blushed at her husband's answer. She could only imagine his thoughts. Hope started to bloom again in Evelyn's heart.

"Oh, my," gushed Gemma.

"Then he apologized for his treatment when we came to visit. And in short, he also apologized for how he pursued us during the house party. Then he admitted I was correct in gifting Cobalt to Evelyn only. He offered his full support in caring for the foal. Then he handed me the letter and left with a purpose to his step. The letter you hold can only be good, my dear. That man means to prove to you and everyone else how much he loves you." Charlotte hugged Evelyn.

"Oh, how romantic." Gemma sighed.

Evelyn smiled at Gemma. Her cousin reminded her of Noel. Both were romantics at heart. Could Charlie be correct? Did this letter hold her husband's true desire? If so, why did her hands tremble? She glanced around the room and saw the anticipation in her family's gazes. Charlie's belief in Reese's apologies sounded so strong. Her sister had steered her wrong many times, but never with the purpose of hurting her. No, Charlie only guided Evelyn to find happiness.

Evelyn ripped the envelope open with her own faith as guidance now.

My dearest Evelyn,

There are no words adequate to declare my sincerest apologies for my behavior over the past few weeks. My need for revenge seems so pitiful now. I can only blame my pride on not knowing how to handle the circumstances of my demise. All I can offer you are my actions from this day forth. I hope we can move past the tribulations of our marriage. Yet, I do not wish to forget them. For they woke me to the yearnings of my heart. A heart full of love for you. I have so much to confess, yet I refuse to do so in a letter. I only wish to leave the following words in hopes that you will return to me.

Her kisses concealed her deception,
A deception fueling my need for revenge,

Her revenge stabs me with its double edge,
An edge of remorse now fills my heart,
A heart she holds prisoner.

Yours forever,
Reese

"Oh, my." Evelyn sighed, holding the letter to her heart.

A dreamy expression filled her gaze. Reese loved her. His letter spoke to her soul, echoing his own heartache. It was then Evelyn realized Reese must have read the book of poems she left on the divan in her bedroom. Did he also read her journal at the end? If so, he'd read her every thought and desire.

"Oh, my! Oh, my!" Evelyn kept chanting.

"What? Tell us," Charlie demanded.

"He loves me."

"Is that not what I told you?"

A smile lit Evelyn's face. "Yes, you did."

Charlie smiled smugly, pulling Evelyn into another hug. The other girls gathered around them. Tears streamed along Evelyn's cheeks with happiness. She would miss their everyday love and support, but they would be there for her at a moment's notice, whether to share her joys or heartache. From this day forward, she hoped it would only be with her joys.

Charlie grabbed Evelyn's shoulders. "What are your plans?"

"The same as before. After I talk to Uncle Theo, I shall return home to see what awaits me."

"No matter the outcome, we are here whenever you need us," offered Jacqueline.

"And that is why I love each of you," answered Evelyn.

Chapter Eighteen

Evelyn inched the door open to her uncle's study. She found him sitting in his chair, staring into the fire. Uncle Theo appeared distracted and didn't hear her enter. Even when she called out his name, he didn't answer. It was only when Evelyn stood near him did he raise his gaze with surprise.

He reached his hand out to her. "Evelyn, dear, I did not hear you."

Evelyn squeezed his hand. "I hope I am not intruding."

"Nonsense, you are always welcome. Please sit and keep an old man company."

"Old? Now who speaks nonsense." Evelyn sat down on the settee.

Uncle Theo laughed. "I only speak the truth of your elder."

Evelyn laughed. "A very wise elder."

"I thought so at one time. However, I believe I am left in doubt." He frowned.

"What leaves you wondering of your wisdom?"

Colebourne folded his hands across his stomach. "A foolish attempt I made to play my hand at matchmaking."

Evelyn tilted her head. "Mmm. But you can brag of your success, can you not? Charlie and Sinclair are deliriously happy."

"Yes, they are. While you are beyond miserable."

Evelyn smiled wistfully. "Your description of my mood is rather daunting."

"But the truth, is it not?" Colebourne arched a brow.

"At times, I would say it matches perfectly. However, it is not a permanent state of my emotions. 'Tis only how I have felt during certain instances since my marital vows."

"They are emotions you should never suffer from if the man you married held your heart in the palm of his hands and protected it with his own heart. I had thought Worthington was that gentleman."

"He is." Evelyn protested, coming to the edge of the settee.

He stared at Evelyn in doubt. "If he is, then why have you been near tears since you arrived yesterday? Why did Sinclair inform me of Worthington's cruel words? And why does your husband sport a bruised face, complimentary of his brother?"

"It is as you explained before I left to marry Reese. You told me he would be a challenge and that love is never easy. I have discovered love is a complicated matter where there are no correct paths to take to achieve its outcome. Only the journey filled with twists and turns will make it feel complete. At the moment, we are wandering on a rocky path filled with many ruts. However, I am optimistic that we shall soon find a smooth journey."

"Optimistic, huh?"

"Very." Evelyn's smile portrayed her belief.

Colebourne slapped his hands together. "Excellent. I had hoped you held this opinion."

Evelyn gazed at her uncle in confusion. She thought Uncle Theo held disappointment in her marriage. Instead, he seemed pleased with her declaration. "You wish for my marriage to succeed?"

He nodded. "Yes, and it is the reason I refused Worthington's request to visit with you. I also informed him you will remain at my residence during your stay in London."

"Why?"

"To prompt him to court you. Why else?"

Evelyn's eyes narrowed. "I thought you were pleased that I wished to fix my marriage."

"I am."

"Then why are you refusing him?" Evelyn stared at Uncle Theo in disbelief.

"It is all part of my plan."

"Plan?"

"Yes. I realize there are some quirks to tweak for your marriage to be joyous."

"You mean manipulations," Evelyn muttered.

"However, you wish to call them, my dear." Colebourne smirked.

Evelyn laughed at her uncle, who was mad about matchmaking. Knowing that Uncle Theo wished for her happiness with Reese gave Evelyn the support she needed to proceed.

"I am afraid I must ask you to halt your plans. Thank you for making my dreams come true. Now I must hold them in my own hands to make them a reality. I am returning home. After this conversation is finished, I want no more interference with my marriage. Reese and I must be honest with one another and deal with our problems together."

"If you're sure. I still think that if I …"

Evelyn held up a hand to stop him. "I only want you to say, 'Evelyn, I will support your wishes as you see fit.'"

Uncle Theo smiled. "Yes, exactly what I'd been about to suggest."

Uncle Theo rose and held out his hand to Evelyn. She rose and wrapped her arms around his middle. She knew Uncle Theo meant well. She loved him more than any simple words could say. At her darkest moments in life, he held her, protecting her from further pain. In his eccentric attempt, he'd tried to secure her a future of happiness. However, somewhere it shook with uncertainty. But Uncle Theo could no longer hold her and protect her from harm. No, those arms now belonged to Reese.

Evelyn glanced down at the document torn in two lying on the side table. When she glanced at the bottom of the page, she noticed Uncle Theo's name. On the line below, it stated her husband's name. Each line held no signature.

She pulled away, lifting the paper. As she read, she saw that it was their marriage settlement. Who was to blame for its destruction? "Our marriage settlement?"

"Yes, it was not to your husband's liking."

New doubts started clawing away at the hope in her heart. However, Evelyn tried to keep them at bay until she heard the explanation. "May I ask why?"

"He refused all that I offered, stating he only wished for your love."

"My love?" Evelyn whispered.

"Your love," Uncle Theo confirmed.

Evelyn understood how important it was for her uncle to offer a marriage settlement to Reese. He needed the funds to support his family, not for selfish uses. The refusal of the offer spoke of the depth of his love. A love Evelyn had waited a lifetime for. Even though a spark never struck her before they met, her heart had yearned for Reese for an eternity and would never stop yearning for him.

Evelyn kissed Uncle Theo on the cheek. "Thank you for everything."

"My pleasure." He sat back down with a grunt. "Now I am ordering you out of my home. You are not to return until your husband declares his love. Not a moment sooner."

Evelyn's laughter filled the air.

~~~~~

Before Reese returned home, he had many stops to make. Each one involved Evelyn, except for two of them. He dreaded making the calls, but they were a necessity. If not, doubt would hang over their heads, doubts he never wanted between them. He planned to make them his last two stops for the day. Once he reached home, he hoped Evelyn had returned. If not, he needed to change his plans for the evening.

Once Reese gathered his surprises for Evelyn, he had all of them delivered home, except for the flowers. While most would buy their wives roses, Reese picked wildflowers that grew around the pond on his property. He wanted her to remember that day. Not because of his falsity, but because of the connection they shared.

With dread, he walked up the stairs. Once inside, the butler rushed him up the stairs to his mistress's boudoir. He found Angelica near the window. When she turned toward him, she undid her robe and let it slide off her body. At least she wore a negligee underneath. If not, then his news would make it awkward.

Angelica was a gentleman's greatest dream come true in the bedroom. She was unabashed with displaying her wares. Her negligee always highlighted her generous curves. Even now, Angelica's bosom teased him falling out of her gown, her nipples peeking through. The slits in her gown showcased her long legs. However, it was her glorious mane of red hair that was her greatest asset. It hung down her back and made a man want to plunge his hands in and hold her to him.

"Reese, my love," Angelica purred. "Rumors had reached my ears of your return to town. I have been waiting eagerly for your visit. I have grown so lonely with you away."

Worthington knew her statement to be false. Just as he found pleasure with multiple mistresses, Angelica was no different. That was why breaking off their affair would be easy. She wouldn't make a scene because other gentlemen's offers dangled at the snap of her fingers. When he didn't advance past the door, she realized the reason for his visit. She slid on her robe and tied it before sitting on the chair in front of the mirror.

"I am afraid I must end our arrangement. I have made sufficient provisions to your account."

She picked up a hairbrush. "May I ask why? Do you find fault with the desire we shared?"

"I am now married. And the supposed desire we share is the same desire you share with any other gentleman. I represent the flash of a coin in your eyes," he scoffed.

Angelica ran the brush through her hair, meeting Worthington's gaze in the mirror. "I do not care if you spoke your marriage vows. Even more of a reason to visit. I am sure your wife cannot satisfy your desires as I can."

Worthington clutched the doorknob. "I care and I will not discuss my wife with you."

"Very well. I see I cannot change your mind. However, my bedroom will always be open if your circumstances change."

"They will not," Worthington murmured before leaving.

He rode in his carriage to the last destination before home. This one would be more difficult. Barbara was more possessive than Angelica. She didn't share her bed with another and displayed her temper whenever she learned that Worthington had bedded someone else. Even though he spent most of his time with Barbara, her possessiveness annoyed him. She misunderstood their relationship, always holding out for a marriage proposal. In which he could, if so inclined, since she was the widow of a peer and not a courtesan like Angelica. However, Worthington refused to live with her jealous tirades, nor would he subject his family to them.

The sun vanished against the city's landscape. The golden hues mixing in with the light from the lanterns. Nightfall hovered on the horizon, waiting to indulge in its decadence. When he stepped from the carriage, he noticed the roads were still full of carriages conveying the lords and ladies of London. He wanted to be at home, not dealing with something he should have taken care of as soon as he got to town. But his anger with Evelyn had still consumed him upon his arrival. Then he'd spent the rest of his time before Evelyn's arrival in a drunken state, which had resulted in the fine mess he found himself stuck in now.

Worthington let himself into the house. He didn't own it, but Barbara demanded that he never knock. She had nothing to hide from him. Since it was near the hour for her to prepare for an evening out, he took the stairs to her bedroom. He pushed the door open, catching the maid helping Barbara into her evening attire.

As always, she looked exquisite. Her hair was coiled into a style of elegance, pearls draped her neck, and her dress hugged her curves to perfection. Her bosom was on full display, leaving no one to wonder what charms she possessed. Many times he had witnessed Barbara dress, and then he would dismiss the maid and coax her into a scandalous dance of desire.

Staring at her now, he felt nothing. No spark. No fire. Nothing but wistful disdain. He would miss their friendship, but that would be all.

"Please, excuse us. I will finish buttoning Lady Langdale," Worthington ordered the maid.

The maid left and Worthington moved into her place, sliding one button after another. She turned in his arms, and Worthington dropped them to the sides, refusing to hold Barbara. He should never have offered to play lady's maid, but he needed the maid to leave. He wanted to break it gently to Barbara. While he'd been direct with Angelica, Barbara would require kid gloves to handle the end of their affair.

He took a step back. But that wouldn't deter Barbara. She started unbuttoning his coat.

"Why finish with my dressing when you are only going to spoil it with your passion?" Barbara purred.

Worthington clasped Barbara's hands to keep her from undressing him. He took another step back, holding her at arm's length. Her enthusiasm turned to confusion. She tried to pull her hands away, but Worthington tightened his hold. He knew once he uttered the words to end their affair, she would unleash her claws.

"We need to talk."

Barbara tilted her head. "What has happened to your face?"

"A brawl."

"With whom?"

Worthington sighed. "Graham."

"Why? What trouble has he caused now?"

"None."

She peeled her hands away and urged him to sit. "I will order a poultice to bring down the swelling. You poor dear. You must bring Graham under control before you cannot."

Barbara flittered around the room, placing items in her reticule, and gathering a shawl from her wardrobe. Once she had the items she needed upon departure, she made her way back over to Reese. He should have known Barbara would try to sit on his lap. He kept trying to work up his nerve to tell Barbara the truth. Every scenario ended the same: with Barbara in a fury.

When she lifted his hand to press against her breast, he jumped, knocking Barbara onto the floor. He remembered his fury when Graham touched Evelyn. He imagined how this scene would hurt Evelyn if she witnessed the exchange.

"Reese," Barbara whined.

"Sorry, sorry," Reese muttered, running his hand through his hair.

He stood rigid when Barbara's hand slid up his leg. He knew the directions of her action. At one time, he would have savored the pleasure of her mouth on his cock, but now he only felt disgust. Before he could stop her, she palmed him, stroking his cock. At least his body didn't betray him.

Barbara's eyes narrowed, her confusion changing to annoyance. When she squeezed harder, Reese winced. He swatted her hand away and moved to the door. He needed to end this. Reese couldn't draw this out any longer. The result would be the same. They were over. Reese wanted to return home to Evelyn.

"I wanted to break this to you gently, but there is no easy way. Our relationship has run its course."

Barbara took a step forward. "Does this have anything to do with your altercation with Graham?"

"In a way," Worthington winced.

"Why are you throwing me over?" She clutched at her pearls.

"I have recently married."

"Married?" Her deathly whisper crawled up his spine.

Reese retreated up until his back hit the door.

"When?"

"A few weeks ago."

"To whom?" Barbara demanded.

"Her name is not important. I will never give her reason to doubt my faithfulness."

"You promised."

He shook his head. "I made no such promises."

"You implied."

"No. You assumed."

"Tell me her name. It is not as if I will not learn who your wife is by the end of this evening," she pleaded.

Worthington puffed out his chest with pride. "Evelyn Holbrooke."

"The Duke of Colebourne's niece?"

"Yes."

Barbara's gaze narrowed. "This makes perfect sense now. Were you not invited to his house party? Did he force you to marry the chit?"

Reese hesitated for a second too long. Barbara caught his waver and came to her own conclusion. It didn't matter how they wed, only that they were. Before he ever took a bride, he'd made a solemn vow to never treat his wife the way his father had treated his mother, and that included taking mistresses. While he had failed with his earlier behavior, he no longer would. The rest of his days would be full of Evelyn by his side, and he would no longer warm another lady's bed.

"The details of my marriage are mine alone. I had hoped we could end this amiable."

Barbara slapped her hand on the vanity. "For the past three years, I waited for you to make me your bride. I rejected other offers for you."

Reese shrugged. "You should never have done that."

"I waited for you," she whined.

"Again, your fault, not mine."

Barbara screeched. "You are a philandering rake."

She lifted a hairbrush off the table and threw it at his head. He ducked, then threw the door open to make his escape. He ran along the hallway, down the stairs and reached the foyer with Barbara following on his heels, throwing whatever object she encountered. Her volatile temper sent the servants into hiding.

Barbara's cries echoed along the hallway. "Please stay. Do not leave me."

To avoid any further outbursts, Reese needed to make it to the safety of his carriage. Barbara would never take this past her front door. She avoided scandals like the plague. Nor would he have to worry about her confronting Evelyn. No, Barbara would dust off her pride and move on. But before she did, she would make it miserable for Worthington.

She reached him at the door and clung to him. Her heavy perfume billowed around them. She tried to draw him into a kiss, but Worthington turned his head to the side, avoiding her lips. He reached behind him, turning the knob. Once he had the door ready to open, he untangled himself from her clutch.

"Take care, Barbara."

He strode down the walk and entered his waiting carriage. He glanced out the window and watched Barbara slam the door in fury. Worthington breathed a sigh of relief at his swift escape. He rubbed his hands together in anticipation for his last stop of the evening. Or at least he hoped. He prayed Evelyn had returned home. He lifted the flowers to breathe in their fresh scent.

Chapter Nineteen

Evelyn returned to an empty house.

She expected Reese to be waiting. Instead, only silence greeted her. She hurried to her bedroom to change her clothes. She had borrowed a dress from Jacqueline, but her older sister was a few inches taller than her. Evelyn kept tripping on the trim. Once she changed and Sally styled her hair, Evelyn went to the window to watch for Reese's arrival.

Evelyn had sworn to make Reese suffer for his cruel words, but she didn't want to play any more games. She wanted their marriage to begin anew, starting this evening. She wondered if Graham could be persuaded to stay at his club for the night. Evelyn wished to have the townhome to themselves.

When Reese's carriage pulled in front of their home and he exited carrying flowers, Evelyn knew Reese thought along the same lines. Before he could reach the stairs, Graham came hurrying up behind Reese and started arguing with him. She couldn't make out their quarrel from where she stood.

Evelyn hurried down the stairs, wanting to stop another altercation. She didn't need Graham to defend her any longer. By the time she reached the bottom of the stairs, Reese and Graham had closed themselves off in Reese's study. Evelyn pressed her ear against the door to listen to the argument.

"Why did you pay a visit to those women?" Graham snarled.

Evelyn froze.

"To end my affairs with them. They deserved to hear of my marriage from me, not the gossip mill."

"Neither one of your mistresses deserved an explanation. The only lady who deserves your attention is Evelyn."

"I disagree," Worthington objected.

Evelyn gasped. She clutched her chest as she felt another betrayal pierce through her heart.

Evelyn opened the door and stepped into the room quietly. Neither of them noticed her entrance.

"Are you mad?" Graham asked.

"No. They each deserved to hear the truth."

Graham stared at Reese with disbelief. "Mistresses do not care because they are already spreading their thighs for another."

"Angelica maybe, but not Barbara."

"No, she only waited for your proposal instead."

Reese sighed. "I discovered the full implications of that this evening."

"You are a blind fool, brother. That has been her intent since you seduced her with your scandalous ways. Her marriage to Langdale never prepared her for the likes of you."

Reese scoffed. "Believe me, Barbara can take care of herself quite well. She does not need your defense."

"No, but Evelyn does."

"No, she does not," declared Evelyn.

Both men stilled, turning in shock to Evelyn standing in the doorway. Reese rushed to her side, carrying the flowers. He handed them to her as if they would alter what she overheard.

Evelyn kept her hands at her side, refusing them. She wanted to believe Reese would never visit his mistresses, but the perfume surrounding him spoke otherwise. The heavy fragrance clouded the distress in his gaze.

Evelyn turned and walked back up the stairs to her bedroom. She didn't wait to hear his explanation. She imagined they could fix their marriage. Instead, she wondered if he had been unfaithful.

"Evelyn!" Reese kept calling her name as he followed her.

Evelyn slammed the door behind her. But that wouldn't keep her husband away. He carried the flowers with him and tried giving them to her. When she refused to take them again, he threw them on the bed.

"Evelyn, please let me explain."

"You have nothing to explain. Do you?"

Reese grabbed Evelyn's shoulders. "Yes, I have much. Will you listen?"

"Do I have a choice?"

Reese sighed. "Yes."

"Can you explain about your most recent visits?"

"To your uncle's home?"

Evelyn shook her head. "No, afterwards."

"Can you be more specific?" Reese winced, trying to draw away from Evelyn's questioning. Graham was right yet again. He didn't have to end his relationships in person. A letter with a token of gratitude would have been sufficient. However, he didn't even want to gift them with anything. He only wanted to shower his wife with gifts. Call it honorable, but he wouldn't treat those women like his father had done countless times.

Evelyn shook off his hold. "Your mistress. Or should I say mistresses?"

Reese ran a hand through his hair. "I wanted to end them with honor. I should have once I reached town, but in my misery, I only drank my troubles away."

"Well, far be it from me to stand in between your lovers. Please continue."

"I do not want any other woman but you, Evelyn."

"The stench draping you speaks otherwise." Evelyn sneered.

"I swear I never touched them." Reese's gaze pleaded with Evelyn to believe him.

"How many did you have?"

Reese winced. "Only two."

"Only two?" Evelyn asked with dismay.

Two too many, Reese realized. He never imagined his visits today would become knowledgeable to his wife. But Graham had seen him leaving Angelica's home and followed him to Barbara's. When he stayed longer at Barbara's, it'd caused his brother to speculate that he hadn't end it with Lady Langdale.

"Evelyn?"

Evelyn pointed to the door. "You need to leave. I would like some time to myself to understand where our marriage stands. I thought I had made a choice, but perhaps I made my decision too swiftly."

"Please, Evelyn," Reese pleaded.

Evelyn turned her back on Reese, expecting him to leave. However, she still felt his presence behind her. The fragrance of his whore stood between them, blocking them from happiness. She tried to trust Reese, but in all honesty, she didn't know the character of her husband, only what she imagined it to be. Their marriage had been a farce since the beginning.

"Reese?" Graham spoke from the hallway.

Reese didn't answer Graham, waiting for Evelyn to turn around. But by the set of her shoulders, he knew she wouldn't. With a sigh, he lifted the flowers off the bed and laid them on the nightstand next to another book. He would leave her once again. However, he would return.

"Evelyn?"

Evelyn turned at Graham's question.

"What can I do?"

She sighed. "I do not know anymore. I returned eager to reunite with Reese. Now I am unsure on where our marriage stands."

"If it is any consolation, I believe he ended those relationships."

Evelyn placed her hand over her heart. "Deep in my heart, I believe he did. However, there have been so many obstacles, demands, and promises that I no longer know if I should trust my heart."

Graham took a step inside the bedroom. "Can I offer my advice?"

"Are you wishing to join my long line of advisors?"

Graham laughed. "That you still have your sense of humor is a positive sign."

Evelyn smiled wistfully. "Your advice?"

"Listen to your heart and your heart only." With a smile of encouragement, Graham left Evelyn to herself.

Evelyn glanced at the flowers. Reese had been so eager to give them to her, and she'd refused them. She walked to the nightstand to gather them. Their heavenly fragrance replaced the scent clinging to Reese. Her fingers caressed the petals. They reminded her of the wildflowers near the pond on Reese's estate, taking her back to a time when their passion had exploded out of control. Instead, that memory represented when he began his deception. Did these flowers represent the same action? Or were they to remind her of a more sensuous memory?

A knock on the door alerted Evelyn to her maid's arrival. She bid her to enter and watched Sally carry in an armful of packages. Sally laid them on the bed, then gushed how Lord Worthington had spent the afternoon visiting the shops to surprise Evelyn with these gifts. The servants had obviously forgiven the earl for his outburst, his tokens of affection for Evelyn winning them over. She dismissed Sally before sitting on the bed to admire the gifts.

Expensive colored paper wrapped each package with a ribbon tied around them for decoration. Ribbons Evelyn could wear in her hair. She smiled at his thriftiness. The first package contained a bottle of her favorite scent. She dipped the sweet fragrance on her wrists and behind her ear.

The next few packages contained books from a variety of bookshops, each one a first edition to add to her collection.

Another gift was from a confectioner. Evelyn opened the container to discover a variety of chocolates. She popped one in her mouth, and the taste of raspberries exploded on her tongue. She moaned in delight at the decadent treat.

Only two packages remained. The first was small and carried the tag of a jeweler, and with it was a letter. Evelyn opened it to read.

My love,

I neglected to provide you with your own ring when we spoke our vows. I hope this ring will do. When I saw it in the store window, it reminded me of your eyes. Emeralds with silver sparks, beckoning me to your side. A spot I never want to leave.

Your love

Evelyn opened the box, and sitting on the plush cushion was a simple emerald surrounded by a dozen glittering diamonds. Each gem sparkled with brilliance. Evelyn slid the ring onto her finger and held her hand out. A smile graced her face at her husband's generosity. His thoughtfulness warmed her soul. All the anger seeped away, leaving her filled with love.

She believed Reese's explanation. She couldn't fault her husband for being an honorable gentleman. While his intentions were questionable, she understood his need not to behave like his father.

The last package contained a silken covering. When Evelyn opened the gift, tears leaked from her eyes. She pulled the garment from its wrapping and held it to her body. Her fingers trailed over the buttons. Her eyes flashed to the vanity and saw her trinket missing. She walked to the mirror to take in the fine detail. Reese had the nightgown she'd worn on their wedding night repaired. She had thought the piece destroyed. But her husband had kept it. Which only meant the pull of their attraction affected Reese deeply.

Images flashed her eyes. The impatience Reese displayed to make Evelyn his on their wedding night. Every kiss, caress, and possession of her soul. Reese might not have known the depth of his feelings for Evelyn then, but this treasure showed off his devotion now.

She shouldn't have sent him away. Everything she said she would do to make their marriage stronger, she'd failed on. At the first obstacle, she'd refused to allow him an explanation. She only hoped he would return soon. In the meantime, she had a plan to put into place. Once he returned, Evelyn would leave Reese with no doubt of her true intentions.

Chapter Twenty

Worthington swirled the liquor around and around. At every spin, he felt himself slipping off the chair. He wasn't, however. Ever since Evelyn had refused to allow him to explain, he'd been drowning his sorrows. Only this time, he didn't remain at home. He'd allowed Graham to take him to their club. After a couple of drinks, Graham had grown tired of watching Worthington drink and took himself off to the game room, leaving Worthington to wallow in his own grief.

However, he wouldn't stay alone for long. Soon two gentlemen sat on each side of him. Worthington turned his head, his eyes lowered, and noticed Sinclair on his left and Gray on his right. He sighed. His evening kept getting better and better, he thought sarcastically. Worthington wondered if Evelyn sent word of his afternoon exploits.

When he looked at them more closely, he realized she hadn't. Instead of fury, their stares were filled with pity.

"Worthington, we would like a word with you," said Gray.

"Bugger off," Worthington slurred.

"We need to discuss Evelyn with you," Sinclair whispered, trying not to draw notice.

"I say bugger off." Worthington's voice grew louder.

Graham walked from the card room to the open area of the club to see Sinclair and Gray flanking his brother. He didn't know what their intentions were, but by the growl of his brother, it wasn't a friendly chat. He needed to convince Worthington to leave before rumors started. From what he'd learned when playing cards, speculations had already formed of Worthington's marriage to the Duke of Colebourne's ward.

When they questioned him, Graham had played the supportive brother, spouting love at first sight and how they couldn't live without one another. However, if anyone took sight of his brother now, they would know that Graham had lied. And if he lied about the status of Worthington's marriage, what else had Graham lied about? He didn't want his fellow peers to question any of his potential falsehoods.

When Graham drew closer, he realized Worthington had kept imbibing. He watched both gentlemen grab his brother by his arms and turn him around. He raised a questioning brow at them, and Gray nodded toward a private room in the back. Graham returned the nod and followed behind them.

However, his brother wouldn't go quietly. He kept arguing loudly, causing heads to turn in their direction. Finally, they reached the Duke of Colebourne's private room, and Graham closed the door for privacy. Inside sat the Duke of Colebourne, nursing a drink. Sinclair and Gray dumped Worthington into a chair. He slumped down, his arms hanging off to the side.

Graham shook his head at his once-proper brother, reduced to a drunken mess. It was usually the other way around.

"Colebourne," Worthington shouted in camaraderie.

Colebourne winced at the loudness. "I take it your reunion with my niece did not go as planned."

"Blundered it, I did." Worthington slurred.

"How so?" asked Colebourne, arching his brow.

"Paid visits to my mistresses." Worthington nodded as if his actions were justified.

"You what?" roared Gray, and Colebourne waved his hand for silence.

"Visited my mistresses, I said."

"May I ask why?" asked Colebourne.

"Tell them finished. No more. Only one woman for me." Worthington waved his hand in the air, emphasizing each reason.

Colebourne nodded. "Excellent."

Worthington shook his head. "Evelyn did not think so."

"She knows?" asked Sinclair.

Worthington nodded, a frown marring his face.

"Oh, you are the most foolish bloke I have ever met." Sinclair laughed.

"How so?"

"Well, there is the fact that you could not distinguish between Charlotte and Evelyn. Then you held Evelyn within your grasp, and you foolhardy visit your mistresses. Fool," answered Sinclair, ticking off the reasons with his fingers.

"However, he recognized the difference," said Colebourne.

"After he married Evelyn," scoffed Gray.

Colebourne took a sip of his drink. "No. Worthington knew the difference the morning after the ball. He might have called her Charlotte, but his heart knew it was Evelyn."

Worthington closed his eyes. He was so bloody tired. He wanted to share a warm bed with Evelyn snuggled against him.

The gentlemen in the room kept chattering about Evelyn and Charlotte. He knew the bloody difference. The duke was correct. He had known the difference since that night. He recalled dancing with Evelyn and escorting her into dinner. When he grabbed her hand, the spark between them had shot through his soul. His body had responded differently than their earlier dance.

While they ate, their passion built to a need out of his control. Their fingers brushed, their whispered words seduced, and desire reflected in their gazes. Worthington didn't need to seduce Evelyn, their desire was mutual. Every moment of their night together seared itself into Worthington's soul. Each caress, each whispered sigh, each kiss, each moan, each joining of their bodies into one, each scream. Pleasure, pure pleasure.

The next morning, as the sun rose, Worthington watched Evelyn sleep and knew who she was. That he hadn't captured Charlotte Holbrooke but her twin sister Evelyn. A rare beauty who also captured his heart. He wanted to react with anger at her deceit, but he couldn't. With Evelyn, a sense of calm always settled over him, and the storm that controlled his entire life vanished into thin air. The only other time he felt this content was when he enjoyed his family, excluding his father.

Even when the crowd gathered in the duke's study, he might have referred to her as Charlotte, but it was Evelyn's eyes he gazed into when he admitted to their rendezvous. Evelyn admitted her wrongdoing with much bravery. While Worthington continued to play the villain. He might have made love to Evelyn, but when he requested Charlotte's hand in marriage, it was to secure a future for his family. Evelyn gave her heart to him, and he was the one who used her for his gain.

"I discovered who Evelyn was before I offered for Charlotte's hand," Worthington admitted.

"Then why offer for Charlotte?" asked Gray.

"Because I needed the funds to support my family, and I wanted that foal for the fortune it would gain." Worthington swiped a hand across his face.

"Selfish bastard." Sinclair sneered.

"That I am."

"God, Reese. You are no better than father. If not worse," Graham said with disgust lacing his words.

Worthington nodded in agreement. "I am afraid so."

Worthington kept agreeing to the slander against him. They each spoke the truth. It wasn't as if Reese didn't carry the shame of his actions every day. He was deep in it. Each time Evelyn pulled him out, the guilt licked at his soul, and he pushed her away. She was goodness to his evil. He didn't deserve her. However, he was a selfish bastard that would keep her.

"And now?" asked the duke.

Worthington sat up straighter in the chair. "I already explained how much Evelyn means to me to you earlier today."

Colebourne narrowed his gaze. "Then why are you here drinking your sorrows? Why are you not pleading your case with Evelyn?"

"She refuses to hear my explanation."

"Stubborn as her sister," muttered Sinclair.

"Yes, those two can try the patience of the devil." Colebourne chuckled.

"Why are you encouraging Worthington's pursuit?" Gray asked his father.

"Because he is her husband, and Evelyn is his wife. That fact will never change. Mistrust clings to their marriage. Until they can be honest with each other, their marriage will flounder. They must admit to their faults and pledge of their love for their marriage to flourish."

The room sat silent after the duke's words. All eyes were on Worthington, waiting for him. He had nothing left to say. He refused to defend himself any longer. The only person who mattered was Evelyn. If he held her forgiveness, then all would be well.

"Are you bloody going to humble yourself or not?" asked Sinclair.

"Yes," answered Worthington, trying to rise from the chair and stumbling forward.

"Perhaps we can be of assistance on helping you to your carriage?" asked Gray.

Sinclair and Gray once again grabbed Reese by the arms as Graham followed. They settled Reese into the carriage, and Graham thanked them for their help. On the carriage ride home, Reese fell asleep, and Graham stared at his older brother while pondering how he'd misjudged him. Their entire life, he had looked up to Reese, never finding him at fault… until their father died, leaving the estate in a crumbling mess with no sight of stabilization. He watched Reese's character change while trying to handle the responsibility. Graham had accused Reese of behaving like their father, but now he realized that Reese was only trying to survive any way he could.

Along the way, Reese's and Evelyn's worlds collided. In Reese's unstable world, he became vulnerable to the emotions Evelyn invoked in him, causing Reese to spin further out of control and react in defense. If Reese were to love Evelyn, then she would be another soul he must protect. His brother thought he failed his family, but the only one he failed was himself by not allowing Evelyn close. Her love could help him fight his dragons.

Once they reached the townhome, Graham shook Reese awake and helped him into the study. He ordered Rogers to bring coffee and keep their return silent. Graham didn't want Evelyn to know Reese was at home until he sobered him. The last encounter with a drunken Reese hadn't gone well. After four cups of coffee, his brother appeared to be his old self.

"Thank you," said Reese, setting his cup down.

"Whatever for?"

"Your bluntness on my behavior and for welcoming Evelyn into our family. I let my jealousy place a wedge between us, for no reason other than I allowed my guilt to rule my judgments."

"I have only ever seen Evelyn as a sister. If you must look for someone to blame, look toward our mother."

They both laughed.

"My own family conspires against me."

Graham smiled. "Only for your best interest. Evelyn is the most amazing gift you could ever receive."

"I agree."

Graham tilted his head toward the door. "Then I will repeat Sinclair's question. What are you bloody well waiting for?"

Reese laughed, rising from the chair. He offered his hand to Graham. Graham clasped it in a friendly handshake. With a nod, they spoke the volume of what they needed to say.

Reese walked slowly up the stairs, rehearsing the speech he'd prepared since Evelyn threw him out. He thought it sounded sincere, but now he doubted himself. Once he reached the landing, his steps slowed even more. Fear ruled his actions now. Fear Evelyn had left again. Fear she wouldn't forgive him. Fear he had ruined any chance at a reunion by his foolish visits to women who no longer mattered.

Fear he'd lost Evelyn's love.

Chapter Twenty-One

When he stopped outside her bedroom door, he noticed the darkness from underneath. He knocked, but there was no answer. Reese pushed the door open and found emptiness. Disappointment set in. She wasn't there.

His steps took him deeper into the room to see that her bedroom sat empty, like it had before she arrived. Evelyn's books were no longer scattered around, and the wardrobe door stood open, showcasing her missing clothes. Not a trace of Evelyn remained.

His heart stopped beating. Despair suffocated him. He tried to claw his way out of the hole, but only sank even deeper. He needed to focus and not let her absence set him back further. It was only temporary. He needed to rethink his plan. Reese couldn't lose her.

He strode through the open door that connected their rooms and stopped when he spotted the single candle burning near the bed. However, it wasn't the candle that halted him speechless. It was the creature lying asleep on his bed. The sensuous siren who caused his heart to beat again appeared innocent in sleep, except for the naked limbs wrapped in a sheet. She was a vision, beckoning him to the tantalizing pleasure they could share.

His glance wandered around the room for a moment before settling on Evelyn again. He saw the flowers in a vase on the fireplace mantle. The divan from her room stood near the windows with her books stacked nearby. Her perfume and ribbons mixed with his hairbrush and cologne. And lastly, the half-eaten box of chocolates rested on the nightstand.

The darkness suffocating him broke open for the lightness shining from Evelyn's silent declaration.

She forgave him.

Every action spoke of her intentions, actions Reese wouldn't deny himself. Evelyn was his salvation. They would spend their life in financial straits, but as long as they were never apart, they would survive life's difficulties together.

Evelyn sighed in her sleep, rolling over. The sheet slipped lower, exposing her breasts. Reese gulped as the creamy flesh glistened in the candlelight. He drew nearer and watched her nipples tighten in the cool air. He longed to draw them into his mouth and savor their sweetness.

Reese sat next to her on the bed and ran his hand down her side. When she didn't awaken, his fingers trailed across her chest, grazing her nipples. Reese lowered his head, drawing a bud into his mouth and sucking softly. Vanilla exploded on his tongue. He moaned his pleasure. He kissed a trail to her other breast, sampling the other nipple. His tongue circled with his teeth, gently pinching the hardened bud.

"Reese," Evelyn whispered, sliding her hands through his hair.

Evelyn pulled his head to her, allowing him to give her pleasure. However, it wasn't enough. He wanted to taste every inch of her. He wanted to savor her on his tongue, inhale her essence, draw the pleasure from her soul into his.

His hands cupped her breasts as his mouth worshipped them. Each tug of his kiss, each lick of his tongue had Evelyn writhing underneath him. Reese trailed fire down her stomach. He pulled the sheet away, uncovering her splendid delights. His thirst doubled at her wetness when she opened her legs. Reese's hands trailed down her legs, then slowly back up, opening her legs wider.

Reese brushed his thumb across her wet core. She squirmed, needing him to ease her ache. To draw out her pleasure, he drew a slow path back and forth. Evelyn raised her hips, pressing herself against his hand. Still, he wouldn't sink his fingers any deeper. His fingers trailed back to her thighs, along her crease, teasing with each delicate touch. Then softly against her curls.

He lowered his head, placing soft kisses where his touch traveled, but not where he wanted to be the most, where Evelyn needed him. With each stroke of his tongue, he built the anticipation. He inhaled her musky scent, losing himself in her hypnotizing fragrance. Reese blew out a soft breath. Waiting. Never moving a muscle. Waiting for the anticipation to consume them. Waiting for her moan.

"Reese," Evelyn begged on a moan.

His tongue struck out and soared a path from the tip of her clit to deep inside, searing her insides with fire on his tongue. Evelyn sunk into his mouth, moaning her pleasure over and over as Reese dominated her senses, taking each sensation and building it to the height of pleasure they never wanted to come down from.

With each caress of his tongue, he devoured Evelyn.

Reese felt Evelyn on the edge, her need building with each motion of her hips. He pulled away and returned his attention to her thighs, to the back of her knees, and then slowly moved back up again. Evelyn moaned her frustration.

With each kiss placed on her body, her need built higher. Reese slid a finger inside Evelyn, and she clenched around him. His other hand rose and twisted her nipples into tight buds. Her body strung tight underneath him. But still, Reese gave Evelyn no mercy. He played her like a violin, sliding another finger inside and creating a steady rhythm with his strokes.

Her moans made the sweetest music. However, her moans were not what he desired to hear. No, he needed her screams to know her devotion. He longed to listen to the sweet melody. He ached to hear his name ring loud and clear of her love.

His mouth clung to her, demanding her release. His tongue devoured her clit as his fingers pulled out her pleasure with a rhythm in time with their hearts. Evelyn unraveled in a rush, exploding under his tongue with a need so powerful, it rocked Reese to his core.

"Reese!" Evelyn screamed.

Reese rose above Evelyn, placing a soft kiss upon her lips. Her sweet smile made Reese's grin grow wider. He brushed the hair from her face. Her eyes lowered.

"I love you, Evelyn."

"I know," she whispered before her eyes closed.

When Evelyn's breathing deepened, Reese realized she had drifted to sleep again. Reese chuckled at how his seduction couldn't keep his wife awake. He rolled off the bed to his feet. He rid himself of his clothes and crawled back into bed. Reese drew Evelyn into his arms and settled her against his chest and pulled the covers over them.

Soon, he drifted asleep with his wife, a smile of contentment on his face.

~~~~~~

Evelyn lifted her heavy lids and peered into the darkness. She heard Reese's heart beating in a slow rhythm against her ear. She smiled, remembering how he had woken her before. He'd done more than awaken her. He'd made her body sing with pleasure. Evelyn melted against Reese, recalling each sensation. Her body hungered for more of his seduction.

Then Evelyn remembered Reese professing his love, and in return, she'd acted the arrogant fool, not responding with her own confession of love. Instead, she'd gone back to sleep, exhausted from not sleeping well over the past week. What must her husband think of her wanton behavior? He'd pleasured her and expected nothing in return. She was shameless… but extremely satisfied. A wicked smile lit her face as she thought of a way to please her husband.

With her fingers caressing Reese as light as a feather, she traced the indentions of muscles in his chest. His firm body invited her need to explore every inch of him. His arms tightened around her, but Reese slept on. Evelyn slipped out of his hold and brushed kisses down his chest and across his stomach.

Before she could move any lower, Reese's arms closed around her and drew her up his body. Her lips hovered over his, their breath mingling together, eagerly waiting for a kiss. She raised her gaze to his and watched the storm brew in his depths. Evelyn lifted a finger to trace across his lips.

Reese's eyes darkened. "Evelyn?"

"Lady Worthington to you, my lord."

Reese's smile turned wicked under her caress, and his gaze flared with passion. He lifted his head to draw her lips into a kiss, but Evelyn pulled back, shaking her head. She lowered and kissed a trail across his cheek, near his ear.

"'Tis my turn to hear you whisper, moan, and scream my name," Evelyn whispered, tugging the bottom of his ear between her teeth.

Evelyn kissed Reese, holding nothing back. She controlled the kiss, taking from Reese what she demanded. She wanted his soul, and she wouldn't stop until she possessed his as he possessed hers. Reese threaded his hands in her hair, holding her to him. Each stroke of their tongues grew bolder with need coursing through their veins. Evelyn's lips trailed away, following the same path from before. Her hands set a trail, and her mouth followed.

She slid between Reese's legs and traced her finger up and down his cock. Her hand replaced her fingers, sliding up and down his hard length in a slow rhythm. It didn't take long for Reese to voice his enjoyment.

"Evelyn," he whispered.

Evelyn's smile turned decadent. Her tongue slowly licked its way to the tip, sliding back and forth, tasting Reese's dew. Her lips drew over him, sliding Reese deeper into her mouth, her tongue guiding him along to pleasure. Evelyn's long tresses caressed his inner thighs as her mouth stole his breath away.

Reese's hands tangled in her hair again, holding her in place. She pulled him out, blowing a soft caress against his hardness. Reese moaned his need. However, he had yet to moan her name. So Evelyn lowered her head and sucked him deeper. Reese throbbed in her mouth, and Evelyn sucked harder, showing him no mercy.

"Evelyn." Reese moaned louder.

Evelyn's hand gripped his cock, guiding Reese in and out of her mouth, her lips dragging up and down to cause a pleasurable friction of desire. Reese's body tensed under Evelyn the closer he drew to exploding. Evelyn quickened her pace, her own body strung with the desire to ignite Reese's passion. He clenched her head to him tighter as he lost control. Reese's body shook when he came undone under Evelyn's heavenly mouth.

"Evelyn!" Reese screamed, his body shaking from the pleasure of her sweet lips.

This time, it was Evelyn who rose over Reese's body and declared her love. "I love you, Reese."

"I know," Reese whispered in awe.

Evelyn laughed at his response, falling across his chest and squeezing him tight. Reese chuckled too, drawing Evelyn deeper into his embrace. He only meant to close his eyes for a second to recover before he made love to Evelyn. Instead, he drifted to sleep again.

~~~~~~

Reese awoke to find his wife propped on his chest, watching him sleep. Her mischievous smile brightened his morning. They had much to discuss, but seeing Evelyn happy brought comfort to Reese. The rest could wait. He wanted to make love to Evelyn. No. He needed to.

Reese slid his hand along her curves, caressing her silky skin. His fingers drifted over the side of her breasts, lingering near her nipples, before continuing their journey. When he slid his hand into her curls, he discovered her already wet and eager for him. His hand explored, drawing out soft whimpers from her. His finger dipped inside, and her smile turned wanton when she pressed herself into his hand.

Evelyn closed her eyes at the sensuous sensation sizzling her core. She pressed her hips against Reese and felt his desire burning his need against her. Before she drew her next breath, he rolled her over and slid between her thighs. With a gentle push, he filled her with his need.

Evelyn's eyes opened to find Reese gazing at her with adoration. He found her hands and linked their fingers together, bringing them over her head. His body danced slowly with hers, drawing out their passion.

Reese lowered his head to draw Evelyn's lips under his. He savored the sweet taste of raspberries from her tongue. Evelyn's moans of pleasure vibrated inside him as she arched her hips into his, drawing out each twirl. He pressed deeper, and her gasp echoed in their kiss. Their bodies grew restless with their need, pleading for release. Reese's mouth devoured

Evelyn's, stealing each passionate kiss from her lips, hungry for more. His strokes grew bolder and deeper. Her wetness clung to his cock.

Reese could no longer control himself. His body sent them flying over the edge with powerful strokes of desire. Their passion erupted around them, their bodies clinging to their love. A love so powerful and deep no one could destroy.

Evelyn clung to Reese, afraid to let go. She never wanted to lose him. Tears leaked along her cheeks. Reese whispered soothing words in her ears. To reassure or comfort Evelyn, she didn't know. She thought she had lost him before she ever really had him. Now that he had given himself to her, she feared he would leave. The love she held for him scared her.

"Evelyn, my dear, talk to me. Tell me your troubles."

"Please, never leave me."

Reese sighed. He feared his need for revenge had damaged Evelyn's heart. He needed to reassure her of his love. No grand gestures would do. Only him speaking from his heart would give Evelyn the reassurance she needed. He only hoped she believed him. He had lied to her too many times before, but these words would hold honesty.

Reese rolled them on their sides, his thumb wiping her tears away. After placing a gentle kiss on her lips, he shared with Evelyn the depths of his own dishonesty and the love he held for her. "My love, I am afraid you are stuck with me for the rest of our lives."

"By choice or force?"

Reese placed another kiss on Evelyn's lips. "Most definitely by choice."

"When did you change your mind?"

"Would you believe me if I told you the first moment you pressed your sweet lips against mine?"

Evelyn scoffed. "No."

Reese laughed at Evelyn's firm answer. "It is the truth."

"Your actions speak otherwise."

"I can see where you might think so. However, it is the truth."

"The first time we kissed, you thought I was Charlotte," Evelyn mumbled, lowering her gaze to Reese's chest.

Reese placed his knuckle under Evelyn's chin, raising it for their gazes to meet. "In which you did not correct me."

Evelyn blushed. "I feared if I did, you would no longer wish to kiss me again."

"However, I did."

"Yes." Evelyn's blush spread along her neck.

"When I coaxed you onto my lap and continued my seduction, I had realized my mistake."

"How?"

"You were shy and never spoke a word. Then I remembered your love of books and knew that your sister would never visit the library in the middle of the night."

"Then why?"

"Deny our attraction and pursue Charlotte at the house party?"

"Yes."

Reese rolled on his back and sighed. "Actions I am ashamed to admit to. My father left our family in financial difficulty. I knew Colebourne's horse was about to deliver a foal that came from a line of impeccable breeding. Charlotte was known to have the ear of your uncle on his horseflesh, so I hoped I could win her over in my pursuit to own the horse. Then when Colebourne dangled a bet before the gentlemen at the house party and offered the foal to whoever could win Charlotte's hand, I thought I had a chance to gain ownership of the horse. To do so, I had to resist you at every chance. You were a temptation I could not allow myself. When I went to collect Charlotte for the dinner dance and you stood there in her dress pretending to be her, my resistance disappeared by your sweet, innocent smile. Then when my gaze connected with yours and I saw your desire, I no longer fought with my control. I had to have you, if only for that one night. When we made love, you brought me to my knees. What I felt for you scared me. I wanted to deny the connection, but I couldn't. I needed you to breathe."

Evelyn rolled onto Reese, propping herself up on his chest. "Then why did you ask Uncle Theo for Charlie's hand in marriage?"

"Because I had already discovered Sinclair and Charlotte's relationship when I visited the stables that morning and knew Sinclair would offer for Charlotte. I wanted to implicate myself and leave no chance for your uncle to deny my offer. If you recall, I did not mention Charlotte's name."

"You only offered for his niece," Evelyn said in awe, remembering the scene in Uncle Theo's study.

Reese smiled. "Yes. If you will also recall, it was you who I focused my attention on. I may have called you Charlotte, but I only played a part for the prize I would receive in the end."

"Then why did you hold on to your anger after we wed? Why did you push me away?"

Reese rolled them over. He tucked a strand of Evelyn's hair behind her ear. "I was furious for myself because I let my emotions come between gaining support for my family. I always promised myself that I would not allow a woman to hold any power over me. Love was not allowed. I watched how it affected my mother my entire life and I did not want that for myself."

"And how is that any different now?"

"Because I cannot live a day without you by my side. I realized that I can no longer deny the depth of love I hold for you. You make my heart complete. I am a mere shell of a man without your love."

"Then explain why you declared your revenge in front of our families?"

"Jealousy."

"I do not understand." Evelyn looked at Reese with confusion.

"I wanted you for myself. When your family arrived and Charlotte taunted us with her gift, I wanted to strike out. Instead, I lashed out at you, destroying the bond we had created. A moment I will regret until my dying day. I thought I could keep you separate the way my father did with my mother, but each day I only craved a lifetime of special moments with you. I hope that one day you will, too."

"There is no need for you to hold out any longer." Evelyn's eyes drifted away.

Reese's hope plummeted before he noticed the smile tugging on Evelyn's lips. When she turned her gaze back, the sparks shot forth, hypnotizing him.

Evelyn placed on her hand on Reese's cheek in a loving gesture. "I have never given up hope since that night a scoundrel seduced me with his scandalous kisses. When he first whispered of his secretive desires and awakened my soul from the shell I hid in."

"My love," Reese whispered before taking Evelyn's lips in the sweetest kiss ever.

When Reese pulled away, Evelyn whispered, "I am sorry, too."

"Whatever for?"

"For deceiving you at the house party. Nothing else. I have not regretted a moment since we left my uncle's estate. But I regret playing you false. I never intended to trap you. I only wanted you to take notice of me."

Reese settled Evelyn in his arms. "Ah, love. I should never have left you to doubt your hold over me. I should have been honest from the start, and then we would not have this clouding over our marriage."

"I feared my defiance pushed you too far."

"Never. However, it took me by surprise. My quiet, sweet, innocent wife refused my orders, provoking an urge to see if she would respond with her threats. In which I can happily say I am more than thrilled with her initiative."

"So it was not what you expected from a dull debutante, Lord Worthington?" Evelyn arched a brow.

Reese laughed. "You are a complete surprise from one moment to the next, Lady Worthington."

"Thank you, Reese."

"For what?"

"For bringing me to life after so many years of feeling dead inside. When I lost my parents, I spent the past few years living in fear, afraid anyone else I loved would die. When you kissed me, it awakened my soul, giving me a reason to live each day to the fullest. Your kisses make me feel alive."

"Then I shall fill every one of your days with kisses." Reese followed his promise with many kisses.

"Only with kisses?" Evelyn whispered.

Reese leaned over and whispered his desires in her ear, promising her a lifetime of seduction. His seductive promises filled her with a desire to make him come undone.

Evelyn pulled back with a wicked smile. "Do you promise to make me whisper, moan, and scream?"

Reese growled, rolling on top of Evelyn and pulling her underneath him. "Louder than you ever have before."

Reese spent the entire day showing Evelyn how much he yearned for her. Desired her. Loved her. Each delectable minute was filled with whispers, moans, and screams, the most pleasurable sounds Reese had ever heard. In return, Evelyn delivered her own revenge, demanding the same. The whispers of their love mingled in between each caress and kiss.

Epilogue

A couple of weeks later, Evelyn and Reese joined their families for a dinner celebrating their Gretna Green nuptials. With a little persuasion, Uncle Theo convinced Reese to accept the marriage settlement he had torn apart. Uncle Theo explained to Reese that the settlement wasn't a result of his dowry for Evelyn, but from the dowry Evelyn's father had written for his daughters before he died. The offering was the last gift from Evelyn's parents and one Reese wouldn't deny. Reese agreed on the stipulation that once their finances were stable, he would return the money to a trust for their future children.

Reese's mother and sisters arrived the day before. They agreed Eden and Noel would have a season. After much grumbling from Maggie, they promised her visits to Tattersalls to overcome her complaints on wearing dresses every day. Reese's sisters soon found themselves swept into Evelyn's family, making quick friends with her sisters, cousin, and Abigail. Her mother-in-law and Aunt Susanna chatted like old friends, making plans for the girls' debuts.

Evelyn watched in amusement as Gemma flirted outrageously with Graham, who did his own fair amount of flirting in return. She looked over to her husband, who was talking with Uncle Theo, and nodded her head to them. He frowned, drawing her uncle's attention. When her uncle showed his displeasure, Reese spoke something to appease him. It would appear

Uncle Theo didn't hold the same opinion as Evelyn that Gemma and Graham made an amazing couple. They had the same hair coloring, and Gemma kept hitting Graham on the shoulder with a friendly gesture. Not to mention the dreamy expression in Gemma's eyes when she gazed at Graham. They were perfect.

"Whatever you are plotting, you must stop now. Your uncle does not approve, nor do I," said Reese.

"I do not plot." Evelyn scoffed.

Reese laughed. "I know better. How else do you explain the reason for our marriage?"

Before Evelyn could answer, Reese snuck them out of the drawing room and into a dark alcove. He dipped his head to steal a kiss. However, one kiss led to another, and Evelyn didn't realize Reese had distracted her.

"The very same marriage you provoked my uncle into demanding?" Evelyn slapped Reese on the chest.

"I plead in my defense the devastating effect of a siren casting a spell on me."

Evelyn's eyes widened. "Are you implying that you became smitten by my very presence?"

"Smitten. Aroused. Loved. Take your pick." Reese stole a kiss.

Evelyn slid her hand inside his suitcoat. "Mmm. I think I may need to hear more of your defense before I state my own."

"Perhaps we should return home before the others to clear any misconception."

"Reese, we cannot leave early. Tonight is in our honor."

"No one will notice." Reese trailed a path of kisses along Evelyn's neck.

"Since this is a celebration of our marriage, I do have a special negligee to wear this evening."

Reese's gaze smoldered at the mention of Evelyn's wedding nightgown. He remembered how she'd rewarded him for fixing the gown he destroyed. Their need to leave became urgent.

"And you do need more practice on your riding lesson."

When Evelyn told Reese how she'd asked Charlotte to give her riding lessons to win his love, Reese demanded that he would be the one to teach Evelyn. Her desire to overcome her fear for him humbled him. He didn't know what he did to deserve this amazing lady, but not a single day went by without worshipping the ground she walked on. Reese had fallen hard for Evelyn.

Reese trailed kisses along Evelyn's neck. His thumbs brushed against her nipples, turning them into tight buds. His hunger for raspberries and vanilla increased his need to seduce Evelyn. Reese's lips hovered near her breasts, his tongue licking the crest between them. He knew it wouldn't be long before she succumbed to his temptation. Reese could be relentless until he won.

"You are shameless, Lord Worthington." Evelyn sighed.

"Only for you, Lady Worthington," Reese whispered.

Evelyn hungered for Reese to appease the ache consuming her body. Her husband had made very valid points on why they should return home. His seduction only emphasized the need for their discussion to continue in the comfort of their bed. No one would miss them. Or else she hoped nobody took notice of their departure.

Evelyn's body warmed from the blush overtaking her senses. She yanked on her husband's hand, and they swiftly made their way to the door. When she looked over her shoulder, Reese was smiling smugly, and she shook her head. Her husband was most sinful. A trait she greatly admired. Evelyn returned his smile with one filled with all her love.

How else was a countess to feel when her earl fell for her?

Look for Gemma's story in
How the Rake Tempted the Lady

If you would like to hear my latest news then visit my website www.lauraabarnes.com to join my mailing list.

"Thank you for reading How the Earl Fell for His Countess. Gaining exposure as an independent author relies mostly on word-of-mouth, so if you have the time and inclination, please consider leaving a short review wherever you can."

Author Laura A. Barnes

International selling author Laura A. Barnes fell in love with writing in the second grade. After her first creative writing assignment, she knew what she wanted to become. Many years went by with Laura filling her head full of story ideas and some funny fish songs she wrote while fishing with her family. Thirty-seven years later, she made her dreams a reality. With her debut novel *Rescued By the Captain*, she has set out on the path she always dreamed about.

When not writing, Laura can be found devouring her favorite romance books. Laura is married to her own Prince Charming (who for some reason or another thinks the heroes in her books are about him) and they have three wonderful children and two sweet grandbabies. Besides her love of reading and writing, Laura loves to travel. With her passport stamped in England, Scotland, and Ireland; she hopes to add more countries to her list soon.

While Laura isn't very good on the social media front, she loves to hear from her readers. You can find her on the following platforms:

You can visit her at *www.lauraabarnes.com* to join her mailing list.

Website: **http://www.lauraabarnes.com**
Amazon: **https://amazon.com/author/lauraabarnes**
Goodreads: **https://www.goodreads.com/author/show/16332844.Laura_A_Barnes**
Facebook: **https://www.facebook.com/AuthorLauraA.Barnes/**
Instagram: **https://www.instagram.com/labarnesauthor/**
Twitter: **https://twitter.com/labarnesauthor**
BookBub: **https://www.bookbub.com/profile/laura-a-barnes**

Desire more books to read by Laura A. Barnes
Enjoy these other historical romances:

Printed in Great Britain
by Amazon

69604791R00139